A Novel

Taken by Mistake

Brianna C. Daring Wyckoff

CONTENTS

1

DETECTIVE/SECRET AGENT JESSE BEST

I shot over a low hill, skidded to a stop, and killed the almost silent motor on my super-powered dirt bike. I shoved the bike to the ground, then threw myself flat on my stomach and covered my head, just before the tremendous explosion erupted and sent everything in a ten-mile radius quaking. When the ground stopped shaking, I raised my head, bringing my night vision binoculars to my eyes. The only thing left of the terrorist bombsite was a deep crater of charred earth and burning rubble.

I grinned at the CBU-89 GATOR bomb. Not a piece still intact.

Headlights speeding toward the ruins from the west alerted me to the danger I was still in. Quickly, I rolled to where I had shoved my bike and righted it. Before jumping on and tearing out of the deadly zone, I turned to make sure the coast was clear. It might be a black night, with no moon or stars and thickly overcast with clouds, but anyone with night vision goggles would be able to see me and sound the alarm.

Several men scanned the area, but none looked my way. Besides, anyone who would come after me if they spotted me no longer had transportation; all the trucks and motorcycles had been destroyed when I triggered the bomb.

However, I still had a good chance of getting a bullet in my back by a sniper rifle equipped with infrared gear. I would have to get out of there carefully and fast. I only had a matter of minutes before the proper authorities came to collect the terrorists, and I didn't want to be around when that happened—too many questions.

I turned to scan the area around me once more, just to make sure no one had seen and followed me after setting the charges. In my line of work, there was no such thing as over-caution. Again, no one, so I straddled my bike seat and gunned the motor.

As I navigated among the low hills and bushes in darkness to minimize the risk of detection, I could hear the roundup back at the ex-bomb site through the tiny radio that fitted snuggly in my right ear.

I'd planted the listening device to stay tuned into the action after I left; I was going to have to write a report on this later.

I rendezvoused with the other six men who'd come along with me on my mission. They'd waited in an army helicopter as my backup, just in case I got into trouble.

We loaded my bike without a sound, and we lifted into the air in less than five minutes. Once we were safely underway, the men wanted to hear how it had gone. It was always like this. Only on very rare occasions was I sworn to secrecy, even among the men who came with me.

I never went on government missions alone, even when only I would be in the action, like this time; it was part of the deal. I never complained; better to have men waiting than no men at all and get stuck as a civilian.

Before telling the men about my mission, I changed out of solid black into more normal-looking clothes, as I would be dropped off directly from the chopper. I couldn't afford to have anyone catch me looking like this. The men knew my routine and simply waited for me to make myself look like a civilian again.

I didn't need a mirror to know how I would look after I was finished. I would change into clothes like those worn by every teenager in the US: dark-wash jeans and a pale blue t-shirt. My blond hair, with its stubborn curls behind my ears, would look neat and in order. There was nothing I could do to make my eyes lose their brightness, but it didn't matter; they were still the same vibrant blue that caught unwanted attention from girls my age. The added brightness would just be more appealing. Lucky me, right?

After changing, I turned to the men. "No hitches." I began. "After you dropped me, I biked into the bomb site, just like we discussed in the briefing. Intel was good. Everything was as they said it would be.

"I took out three sentries without a sound. The fourth saw me, but he's not going to be much of a witness against me – I was faster." The men nodded their heads. Not a topic to discuss over dinner, but in this line of work, not everyone walks away. Had that guy been able to identify me, things would have turned very bad.

"Any trouble with the timing devices?" One of the men questioned.

I shook my head. "After running drills with them for the last forty-eight hours, I'd be disappointed if I had trouble. I planted them and activated them just like I was trained. Once everything was set, I gunned my bike and got out of there." I indicated the ear the listening device had been in before I put it away with the rest of my gear. "The authorities got the tip I called in and finished the wrap-up for me. No one got away." I grinned slightly.

"No one knows how the bomb exploded early, either. They're going with faulty workmanship."

One of the men grinned at me, slapping me on the shoulder. "I guess a little rat must have slipped in when no one was looking and chewed a few wires. Good work, man."

I nodded, accepting his praise but doing nothing with it; I didn't need to make a big deal of things. This was my job. They could appreciate someone who could go on a real-life mission and come back without being hyper and giddy over what he'd done.

But that was me: fourteen-year-old detective/secret agent, Jesse Best.

2

RETURN TO TWIN PINES

I sighed as I fell back onto my single bed, arms spread out in contentment. I may have loved being a detective/agent and the thrill of being hot on the trail of a bad guy, but there was something about coming home that always made me feel warm. Maybe it was that I had solved another case and made the world a little better.

A sadder, darker thought was perhaps the warm feeling was due to the simple fact I *got* to go home. I hadn't been killed during my sleuthing mission, unlike my parents.

The memory of my tall, strong dad and stunning petite mom brought on that familiar ache in my chest that always accompanied thoughts of my hero parents, even though it'd nearly been two years since their deaths.

They had been in the same business as me, which is why I got here in the first place. Dad had been a top-notch private detective, and Mom a fantastic secret agent for the CIA. Both jobs put me in two places. The first was right in the middle of the crosshairs of any bad guy either one of my parents brought down. The second was in a place where crime-fighting surrounded my entire life. It was no wonder I followed their example and became a private detective/unofficial secret agent for the CIA.

Sure, I admit that being fourteen and everything I am (no arrogance intended) seems unreal to people—especially to my employers—but you have to know the whole story to really understand it.

My career started when I was a toddler. A double agent that Mom had busted decided to get back at her by hiring a sniper to take potshots at her one-year-old son: me. It was then that my parents laid out my life's plan for me. I would simply have to be molded into the youngest, most diligent detective/agent ever to walk the earth.

(In case you're wondering why I keep writing detective/agent, it's because they couldn't agree on which they were training me for. To keep the peace, I've simply never aligned myself with one or the other, considering myself equally both. Back to the recap.)

There had been no other solution to keep me safe from their enemies, so I began my training in martial arts when I was just two years old. When I was little, I never went to a real school because my parents decided to train me at home, making sure I got the right training for my career. They didn't do it alone. By the time I was five, I knew several dozen detectives and secret agents by their first names.

I want to set one thing straight right now—my parents only laid in me the foundations of being a detective/agent. I had been the one to beg and plead to be able to really use my training against bad guys. It had been my decision, and I have never regretted it—not even after Mom and Dad died during a joint mission, leaving me alone.

A knock sounded on my door, interrupting my line of thought. Using my foot to kick the duffle bag I had yet to unpack under the bed, I sat up and called, "Who is it?"

"It's me, dear, Miss Daisy," came the muffled reply.

Smiling, I invited her in.

The door opened, and in stepped short, plump Miss Daisy. She and her husband, Mr. Ace, were my Floor Parents, and they always fussed over every boy on their floor as if he were their very own—all the Floor Parents did; it was one of the things that made Twin Pines Home for Teens such a great place. Much better than foster care, that's for sure.

Miss Daisy had snowy white hair cut in a bob hairstyle around her face and sparkling green eyes, even if she was approaching sixty-five this coming October. She always wore fiery bright colors; I never once saw her in anything drab.

She closed the door before coming over to sit on the bed next to me. "How was your mission, Jesse?" Miss Daisy and her husband were the only two in the entire home who knew I was a young detective/agent.

I told her all about my mission, leaving nothing out; it was another part of the deal. Miss Daisy and Mr. Ace were sort of my handlers. I told them everything, and they helped cover for me.

When I finished, her face was flushed with excitement. "Oh, for the days when I was a young agent myself! I used to love the thrill of being in danger and just getting out of traps before they were sprung."

I cocked an eyebrow. "You liked being in danger?"

She laughed and put her arm around my shoulders, giving me a squeeze. "You better believe I did, and you do, too. Otherwise, you wouldn't have stayed in this business so long."

I smiled and had to agree. There was just something about having a sniper breathing down my neck that exhilarated me. It wasn't natural to thrill at something so deadly, but when I had been dodging bullets all my life, I guess it just sort of affected me that way. It was that or freak out and get out, and I loved what I did too much for that.

"I thought I might warn you while I'm here—your old Twin Pines enemy is back," she warned.

"Luis Smith?"

She nodded. "With threats to see you in Twin Pines nurse's office because you turned him in for stealing that camera."

"Thanks. I'll make sure I don't get stuck in any classes with him—the last thing I need is my life here to get exciting by having fireworks planted in my desk."

"You just be careful. You're supposed to be an easygoing boy as Jesse Target, not a fourth-degree black belt."

Target is my legal last name; Best is the codename I was given when I aced a mission everyone claimed only the "best" could pull off. Having two separate identities helps protect me, too. None of my enemies comes knocking on my door because no trails lead from Jesse Best to Jesse Target. "I know. I'll be my old self, despite Smith."

She pulled several sheets of paper from her clipboard and handed them to me, telling me what each one was as she did. "Here are the activities that will be going on this month, and here is your school schedule. There are also a few things in there that you might want to know happened while you were gone."

I skimmed them all, planning to go back and read them later in more depth. "Thanks, Daisy." No Miss before her name—she had strictly told me that I was simply to call her Daisy when we were alone: one agent to another.

"You're welcome," she told me. "I'll leave now so you can unpack everything before supper. As you can see, it will be served early tonight."

I unpacked quickly, eager to take another long look at the three sheets of paper. A couple of activates really got my attention.

One was adoption day—not that many of us teens were ever adopted, but sometimes people did want teenagers.

I would, of course, be sick for that day—I wasn't supposed to be adopted. Life was perfect for me in this place. I could slip in and out when cases came without anyone really suspecting. If I were ever to be adopted, everything would possibly fall apart. I would either have to tell my new parents about my work, or simply disappear and reappear whenever I had to. Very tacky. No, it was just better never to get near respectable parents looking for a teen to adopt.

Not that I minded too much. I had had a great thing with my family, and I knew no matter how great the next one could be, it would never be like my birth family.

Another activity that got my attention was the announcement that on August 23rd, the big donors to Twin Pines would be coming to visit and see what their donations were doing. One name caught my eye above all the rest: the Taylor family. They were the biggest donors of them all. It was rumored they really owned Twin Pines and only pretended to be donors for some strange reason. I was interested in meeting that family, if just by passing them in the hall.

The bell rang for supper, so I had to put aside my school schedule until afterward. I joined the rest of the boys filling the hall heading for the big cafeteria. No one noticed I hadn't been doing this for the past week—that was the best thing about being in a big place.

That night, I stayed in my room, writing my mission down in the thick book I had kept since my first case. Someday, I would be free to talk about them, and I would tell them to my kids if I ever had any—you never know, but one might want to be a detective or secret agent, like me.

There was a knock on my door, then Ace, Daisy's husband, called, "Two minutes till lights out!"

"Thanks," I called back. I put my book and pen away under my bed with the rest of my things, then I turned off the light and snuggled under the covers. My last thought before slipping off to sleep was, *Wonder when the next call will come?*

3
BRUSH WITH TROUBLE

School started the next day; I had come back just in time. Studies were easy for me because I had been trained since my toddler days to listen closely and remember what I heard. It was all part of being an agent or detective.

Some would say I lucked out. Me? I say God was helping me to protect my secret identity. I didn't have a single class at the same time as Luis Smith. There went some of my worries. Keeping my cover with a 185-pound sixteen-year-old punk ready to squish my lesser 125 pounds into goo was tough; not having to plan a hop-dance around him during classes made it easier to keep playing the master roll of Jesse Target.

I could avoid Luis out on the basketball court or in the swimming pool, but stuck in a deck having to listen to the teacher while getting my backbone crushed by Smith did not appeal to me.

I know what you're thinking. I've made myself look something like a first-class sissy who has to take being bullied by punks. But that's not Jesse Target any more than it is Jesse Best. As a rule, Jesse Target is an easygoing, polite boy. But to every rule, there's an exception. Sometimes, even a tolerant boy such as Jesse Target loses his temper, and the avoid-a-fight-if-at-all-possible kind of kid turns into an angry, fist-clenched avenger.

Like when Luis stole newcomer Tommy Shaw's camera and made him cry because it had been given to him as a last gift from his parents.

Okay, so maybe the fight had been avoidable, but Luis had made me so sick over the months that the Jesse Best side of me had momentarily taken control. I hadn't blown my cover by using any karate moves, but I did make myself an eternal enemy—Luis Smith never forgave anyone.

The first week of school flew by, and it was August 23rd before I had even fully gotten over the letdown I always had after returning from being the thrilling Jesse Best to normal Jesse Target. But not even adrenaline letdown would stop me from enjoying this day.

I had no idea why today felt so exciting. It was only Donor's Day. Maybe it was because the parents had wanted to bring their kids along this time to show them just how blessed they were to still have parents.

Some of the guys planned on giving the sons gruesome stories about their lives before coming to Twin Pines. Others planned on hamming off for the daughters. I just wanted to get a look at the children of the people who willingly gave to this foundation.

I wasn't sure which outfit I wanted to wear. I had two I liked and thought were appropriate for the occasion. I finally chose a pair of black jeans and a red t-shirt and pulled on my black high-tops, cringing when I saw the outer part of the toe and the repair I had made with black magic marker. Then I got up and looked around my room.

It was a Jesse Target room. Neat, clean, filled with model airplanes and other normal Christian fourteen-year-old stuff, and not a hint of detective or agent things to be seen. I didn't even have my mystery books on the bookshelf, but had placed them with the rest of my Jesse Best things in the secret compartments I had created—cleverly, I might add, by prying up several floorboards all over the room, where they wouldn't be noticed. There was only one thing about Jesse Target's room that would resemble Jesse Best's: the tidiness. Other than that, the resemblance was rather slim, and that's the way I liked it.

I smiled as I headed to the great assembly room where all the teens had been requested to gather at ten o'clock that morning.

"By the time I'm through with you, Target, you'll look just like the Cheshire cat to match that ridiculous grin!"

Why didn't I realize he was waiting to get me on a day like today? I miserably wondered as I looked around. It should have been obvious! A boy like Smith doesn't wait to get even unless he thinks he can gain something by it. Beating me up on Donor's Day sure will gain him publicity, which is all he wants.

"Luis. Jesse. You are going to be late to that assembly if you don't put a scoot on it," Ace's clear voice warned.

We both looked to see him and Daisy coming towards us, smiling brightly as though neither suspected what had almost happened.

Coming up to us, Daisy linked arms with me while Ace put a hand on Luis's shoulder. "Come on, boys. We don't want to miss the opening of Donor's Day."

As we walked, I gave Daisy a thanks-I-owe-you look. She shook her head and laughed. I knew my debt was canceled.

4

FACE TO FACE

The assembly was just the normal be-on-your-best-behavior speech that always came before anything like Donor's Day. Of course, it did save me from having to decide whether or not to escape Luis' payback. After the assembly, everything went as it did on a normal day until the donors arrived with their kids.

Every teen in Twin Pines stood on tiptoe or climbed a tree to get a glimpse of the wealthy kids. All but me. I tried, but Luis kept between the crowd and me. If I were to get a good look at them, I would have to catch them in the halls. I turned away and disappeared, while Luis looked the other way.

I tried several times to see the Taylor family or any of the donors, but other kids flocked to them each time, blocking my view.

If I didn't know better, I thought with a shake of my head after the fourth time I was blocked out. *I'd say they've all ganged up on me in a conspiracy to make sure I never see the donors' kids.*

I decided to stop trying so hard. Maybe that would work better than killing myself to catch the tiniest glimpse. It seemed to always work in books or on T.V—maybe it would work for me, too.

Or maybe it won't, I thought glumly three hours later. *The families have finished their tour and will be leaving soon, and I didn't get any closer to seeing them by* not *trying than I did when I was* trying.

I sighed and pushed my hands into my pockets as I walked up the flight of stairs that would lead to the hallway going to my bedroom. *Maybe I can try again next Donor's Day. They won't have their kids with them then, though, and I've already seen the adults.*

Three stairs from the top, I heard a commotion coming from the hallway I was about to enter. It sounded like a heated argument, so I took the last three steps in one and rounded the corner to see what was going on.

Why aren't I surprised?

It was Smith. He must have decided to beat up some other kid since I had managed to evade him all day. He was about thirty feet down, facing the left-hand wall and leaning against it, his arms on either side of the boy he had trapped. I couldn't see the victim's face.

I stayed where I was, not sure what I would do. Jesse Target would go back downstairs if the commotion didn't seem too violent. If the victim could really get hurt, Jesse Target would charge in and do his best to rescue him without blowing Jesse Best's cover. This case promised to be the latter.

I came closer, listening for the other boy to see which one had been snagged by the bully. If the victim was another bully, I would probably let them fight it out—two bullies wouldn't get half as hurt as one bully and a normal kid, and I didn't want to become too aggressive as Jesse Target.

I paused when Luis finally stopped ranting long enough so that I could hear the other boy speak. "Look, I don't know who you are," he was insisting in a very familiar tone. "I don't live here—I live with my family, the Taylors. You know, one of the donors."

My eyes popped wide. Smith had decided to pick on one of the donor's kids? Did he have to choose the Taylors' only child? Did he want us all to get thrown out on the street when the Taylors found out and withdrew their donations? What was he thinking?

The Taylor boy's next words really got my attention. "I'm not Jesse Target; I'm Philip Taylor! I don't know what you have against Jesse, but you don't have to take it out on me."

Why would Taylor say that? I wondered as I crept forward. This was definitely a fight even Jesse Target would break up. *Has Smith said something about not being able to find me, and that's how he explains this idiotic action?*

Smith laughed mirthlessly. "Give it up, Target; you can't bluff your way out of this. I'm going to clean your clock for ratting on me!" He brought his fist back and was really going to hit Philip, but I grabbed his arm and yanked him backward.

"What are you doing, Smith?" I cried in what sounded like shock mixed with anger, which was exactly what it was. "You trying to get us all thrown to the wolves?" I dropped his arm but didn't turn to look at Taylor—better to keep my eye on the boy who would try to pulverize me.

Smith stared at me as though I'd grown two heads and four arms. He squeezed his eyes closed, rubbed them, then opened them again. "Jesse Target?" He asked, squinting a little.

I crossed my arms. "Who else would I be? What do you think you're doing, beating up one of the donor's kids? What's your problem?"

For the first time ever, Luis was completely speechless. Finally, he managed to squeak out, "You're Jesse Target?"

"Yes, I already told you—"

He cut me off. "How'd you manage to look like that?"

I gave him a puzzled look. "I look just like—"

"Him!" Smith cut in for a second time. His voice and face were full of shock. He was pointing at Philip Taylor.

I followed the pointing finger to where the Taylor boy still stood, his back against the wall. I froze. No one spoke or moved, not even Luis.

I looked at Philip, and Philip looked at me. I couldn't believe what I was seeing; Philip's expression matched my own— unbelieving. Very hesitantly, I reached out my right hand to touch Philip's face, just as Philip reached out his to touch mine. Automatically, we jerked our hands back, but that mirrored action only made our eyes grow wider.

Smith was the one to break the silence. "I don't understand!" He complained. "There are *two* Jesse Targets?"

Neither of us answered; we were too busy looking the other one over.

Looking at the boy before me was like looking in a mirror. He was my size and height, he had bright blue eyes identical to mine, and he had my blond hair. He even had the stubborn curls behind his ears that my hair had!

If that wasn't shocking enough, we were also wearing the same outfit. I could understand everything but the outfit—I know everyone in the world was supposed to have a lookalike, but I didn't think in a million years the lookalike wore the same kind of clothes and on the same day. We were perfect replicas. No wonder Luis mistook him for me.

We could have stood there forever, just staring at each other, but Mrs. Hoffman, the head administrator's wife, came up the steps calling, "Philip? Philip Taylor! Your parents are ready to leave now. Where are you?" She spied us and came over. Luis's thick torso shielded Philip, so she didn't see him. "Philip, everyone was worried. Some of the girls in your party even fainted; they thought something horrible happened to you." She took my arm and started to take me back toward the steps.

"Wait, Mrs. Hoffman!" Smith cried, pointing behind him to where the real Philip still stood. "This is Taylor. *You* got Jesse Target."

"Jesse Target?" Mrs. Hoffman repeated. I wasn't one to get in trouble a lot, so she didn't know me.

Smith explained, "He's one of our boys."

Now Mrs. Hoffman laughed. "Very funny, Luis. This is Philip Tylor." Then her eyes narrowed. "I want to see you in my husband's office after the donors leave." He was going to be in trouble for this.

When she started to leave, still holding my arm, Smith leaped around her and insisted, "Look!" He pointed to the still frozen Philip

Mrs. Hoffman turned her head, then blinked several times. She looked from me to Philip. "What on earth...?"

Smith took my arm and tugged me to stand side by side with Philip. He stepped back, and his eyes became even round-er, while Mrs. Hoffman gasped. "I thought I was mixed up," he said in amazement, "thinking they looked alike while standing apart, but now I know my eyes aren't lying. They're identical! I can't believe it! Wait till I tell everyone Jesse Target looks just like Philip Tylor!" He turned and ran down the hall.

Mrs. Hoffman found her voice; it seemed everyone but Philip and I could find their voice. "I, I don't know what to say! You two are identical, truly identical. I can't believe it!"

I turned to take another look at him, only to find he had done the same thing. He even moved just like me! This was too creepy. I could feel my skin start to tingle. I moved to rub my arms, but Philip did, too!

He returned my wide-eyed stare with one of his own. We both shook our heads, denying what we were seeing. At the same beat, we turned and ran in opposite directions. He ran for the stairs, and I ran for my room.

When I got there, I slammed the door closed and leaned my back against it, panting. I shook my head. That hadn't just happened. There was no way a person could show up one day and be another me. It just wasn't possible! Unless there were clones, but I knew better than that.

So, what is it? A trick by one of my enemies? I shook my head as I sat at my small desk. That didn't make sense. Why send a boy who looked like me and not an assassin? *There's something weird going on, and I'm going to find out what.*

5
INVESTIGATING

I fell asleep that night over my laptop keyboard.

Not given the privilege to wallow in the shock of meeting my mysterious replica, I'd locked my door, gotten out my Jesse Best stuff, and went to work, hitting all the information highways accessible to me. I also called up my informants to see if there was word of something going down concerning Jesse Best.

When I woke the next morning, Daisy and Ace were by my side. "Hi, Jesse. Working late, I see," Ace said with a smile, then added seriously, "It's a good thing not everybody can get into your room, or you would've been sunk."

I rubbed my face to wake up a little more and looked around. The place looked like a field base, not a 14-year-old's room. "I must have fallen asleep," I apologized.

"I'd say so," Daisy agreed, looking at my things. "What were you looking up?"

I covered a yawn. "I was making sure no one had linked Jesse Best with Jesse Target."

"What made you think they had? None of your enemies have gotten a good look at you to be able to identify you as Jesse Best, let alone to link him with Jesse Target."

"True, but I was just trying to figure out what happened yesterday."

"Did something happen that you didn't tell us? Do we need to get you out of here?" They were worried.

I shook my head. "No, nothing like that…. Philip Taylor and I, well, we look alike. *Exactly* alike."

They seemed relieved. "We heard about it. The whole place heard about it."

"Luis," I said with disgust. I'd known he'd blab it to everyone, but it didn't change how I felt about it.

"That's right," Ace confirmed.

"Why do you think that means someone found you?" Daisy asked.

I shrugged. "How else can I explain it? I mean, he was like my clone or something! No one could be that much alike without something going on. Right?"

The pair looked at each other but didn't answer my question.

I frowned. "What?"

Daisy answered. "Maybe what you're looking for has nothing to do with your secret life. Maybe there's a different explanation for it."

"What do you mean?"

"You've put two and two together before, Jesse," Ace told me softly. "Do it again now."

"What do you mean?" A feeling in the pit of my stomach told me I wasn't going to like where this was heading.

"According to Luis, you two looked the same, acted the same, and were dressed the same," Daisy said, giving me a push in the direction they wanted me to go.

I crossed my arms, feeling my face flush with anger. "Are you saying what I think you are?"

"Only one kind of person does that, Jesse."

"How can you even think that?" I exploded. "It's ridiculous!"

"Despite people's greatest efforts, humans are yet to be cloned. What other explanation is there that's logical?"

"He's not my twin, okay?" My voice was sharp—sharper than I had ever spoken to them before. "You knew my parents. You knew them even before I was born. You know they only had one child—me." I turned my back on them, smashing some keys on my keyboard. None of my fingers were on the right keys, so instead of writing words, it looked like a two-year-old was trying to type. With a frustrated sigh, I erased what I'd written.

"Calm down, Jesse," Ace told me, placing a hand on my shoulder. "You know the drill: take a deep breath, exhale two-thirds. Do it again." He repeated it until I obeyed.

It helped. It was something my mom had taught me. Whenever I was overwhelmed, instead of counting to ten, I controlled my breathing.

"Okay," Ace told me when he was satisfied. "Now, tell us what you think about this."

I turned to face them. I shrugged a little. "An enemy?"

They looked at each other in that husband/wife way, seeming to discuss what I'd said without a word. Ace turned back to me. "What would sending a boy that looked like you gain?"

I shook my head. "That's what I'm trying to figure out." I looked from one to the other. "He's not my twin," I insisted, this time in a more controlled voice. "He's not. How could he be? They wouldn't give me up for adoption, so why would they give him up?"

The pair looked at each other again. This time, Daisy spoke. "You're right,"

I gave them a suspicious look. "Do you know something I don't?"

"No, there's no secret. At least, none any of the agents or detectives know about."

I let out a relieved sigh.

"We'll see if there's some kind of explanation out there, Jesse," Ace promised.

"I alerted all my informants; I should be hearing back from them sometime today." I turned back to the screen, but Daisy shook her head.

"First, you go to school, then you hit the highways again."

"But Daisy," I protested as Ace pulled me from the chair and sat in it himself, while Daisy pushed me into the small bathroom. "I can't go to school right now!"

"Ace and I will keep looking while you're in school," she firmly told me while tossing a shirt at me that muffled my protests. "You have a cover image you have to portray, and you can't let it go—especially after the commotion yesterday caused."

"Commotion?" I asked, looking in the mirror to comb my hair.

"Yes. Luis could become a very good broadcaster." She made her voice mimic a broadcaster's. "Philip Taylor and Jesse Target: identical!" She dropped her voice back to normal. "Everyone's eager to ask you about it; you can't disappear right now. You're popular—you have to go out there and play Jesse Target. Ace and I will hold down this side of the fort while you hold down the other."

"All right, but don't get too mad at me if I don't learn much."

A wave of teens smashed into me the minute I left my room. Everyone spoke at once. "Is it really true you and Philip Taylor look alike?" came from one direction, while from the other came, "Luis said you two copied each other's every move, like you were one person!"

I shrugged to the teens around me and simply said, "It's true," and tried to continue to the cafeteria where we would eat breakfast before starting school.

The teens flanked even tighter. "Well, what do you have to say about it? Don't you find it weird?"

I offered an indifferent shrug. "It means nothing. Everyone in the world has a lookalike; mine just happens to be filthy rich."

"Not so fast!" The kids objected as I tried to push through them again. At this rate, we'd never get to the cafeteria, and we'd all get tardy marks on our report cards.

"I've met my lookalike," one boy declared loudly. "And he and I didn't act anything alike. We only looked the same. We didn't *dress* the same. There's something weird about this."

I wasn't going to get into another discussion about it, so I reminded them of the consequences of being tardy. "Guys, we're going to be late to school if we don't hurry. I, for one, don't want to get my knuckles rapped."

"Ah, you know they don't allow rapped knuckles anymore; they just give us dumb assignments."

"Have you forgotten Mr. Alegohopher? Rumor has it he rapped Tommy Crenshaw's knuckles just last month. You want to see if the rumor is true?" I pushed by them, but they stuck to me like electricity sticks to wire.

When we got to the cafeteria, things only intensified. Daisy was right—I was suddenly the only Mr. Popular anyone saw. Everybody had to come to ask me about Philip and my similarity.

It was a good thing I had been grilled to perfection about handling this kind of situation. To a "normal" kid, all this sudden attention would either go to his head or make him crack and run away. I was able to coolly, yet with just enough embarrassment to satisfy Jesse Target, answer all the questions, and handle the intense attention.

It's a good thing nothing important was talked about today because everyone would have missed it, I thought as the bell rang to dismiss school. *I sure didn't learn anything except that some of the kids have lousy handwriting.* I'd had more notes passed to me than Becky Thompson on Valentine's Day!

I got up to leave the mathematics class but was shoved back into my desk and surrounded once again. You'd think that after six hours of hearing the same thing over and over, these guys would leave me alone. I was finally able to break free and headed for the boys' wing—I had some investigating to pick back up.

I had to fight to get to my door, which I firmly closed and locked behind me. "You'd think no one ever looked like another person before!" I complained to Daisy and Ace, who were still sitting in front of my equipment and working hard on it. "The harassment hasn't stopped all day!"

After neatly putting my books away, I leaned against the chair Ace sat in and asked, "What's come up so far? Anything more than what I already had?"

Ace shook his head. "We've buzzed everyone about what happened yesterday, and they all started to search for an explanation. So far, our results have all been negative feedback. Nothing has made a ripple in the underworld, and believe me, if someone was taking down a big name like Jesse Best, there would be some evidence about it."

"We did a background check on the Taylors," Daisy added. "Nothing suspicious going on there."

"You mean like there was no switch with the Taylors' son?"

"That's right; there's nothing out there."

I refused to accept what they'd apparently already decided was true. "I'm going to keep looking," I told them stubbornly as Ace moved from the chair so I could get in it.

They just nodded. "We'll come by later tonight to see if you've found anything," Daisy told me. "Meanwhile, Ace and I need to show our faces around Twin Pines; we don't want anyone getting suspicious."

As they left, I called over my shoulder, "Make sure you lock the door behind you, please—wouldn't put it past any of them to barge right in without knocking if you don't."

"Will do."

I heard the door shut, and the lock clicked soundly. Leaning over the keyboard to my laptop, I switched from Jesse Target to Jesse Best and got to work. I was still there when Daisy came back that night with supper for me.

"I explained to the cook that you were still a bit shaken up from yesterday's ordeal and all the attention you got today. She took pity on you and decided to make you a tray so you wouldn't have to face the crowd again." Her eyes twinkled as she set the tray beside me. "She really is a sweet thing."

I smiled at her absently as I took a sip of the cool lemonade, never taking my eyes from the lines I was reading.

"Finding anything?" Daisy asked as she sat beside me.

I marked the section in my mind, then tore my eyes from the screen. I shook my head. "Not yet, but I'm still waiting on returns from some of my contacts."

Daisy nodded. I'd worked with her and Ace long enough to know that if they didn't say anything, they disagreed with you.

I frowned. "Daisy, it's impossible that we're twins. Why do you and Ace keep thinking that?"

She sighed and shook her head. "I don't know. I suppose you're right. We shouldn't decide something without evidence, and none says that you are twins, though it does seem like it."

I nodded my head firmly, ignoring the last part. "Good. There's an answer out there somewhere, and we're going to find it."

She ruffled my hair affectionately. "I don't doubt you for a minute, Jesse Best."

It was late by the time Daisy told me we had to turn in for the night. I still had school, and she wasn't as young as she used to be. I agreed, knowing we really had done a lot for one day, even if we hadn't found anything. I shut down all my stuff, stashed it away so no one could find it, and undressed for bed.

Before crawling between the covers, I knelt by the side of the bed and fervently prayed for us to have better luck tomorrow. As I curled up under the blankets, my mind wandered for the millionth time to Philip Taylor; he probably would have been in bed hours ago. For some reason, that thought gave me satisfaction. For once, he hadn't done the same thing I had.

6
SECOND SHOCK

I stayed in the spotlight for the next couple of days, but after Luis Smith beat up Eddy Drummond, he got most of the attention; this made me freer to stay in my room and investigate.

So far, search results had shown that there was no sign at all in the underworld that anything unusual was happening or about to happen. There was nothing amiss with the Taylors whatsoever. There wasn't even anything outside the case. None of this surprised me because of what I found when I hacked into the Taylors' private computer.

The idea had come to me late Friday night. The smartest thing for me to do was hack into the Taylors' computers and see what information I could dig up there. The results of those hours of hacking and reading had been both good and bad.

The good part was that none of my enemies had cloned me, as we'd pretty much already determined, but at least now I knew for sure. The bad part was I had found that Philip Taylor looked the same as me from the time he was an infant to now, which did nothing for my case.

The Taylors had an extensive picture memory lane on their computer. It started with the first date and went through their marriage, Mrs. Taylor's pregnancy, and up to this very day. All the pictures had been carefully dated, and a tiny caption written under all of them.

The result of this discovery? Philip Taylor had always been there. There had been no switch made, no brainwashing, no illegal activity. As weird and unsettling as it was, Philip and I were legitimate lookalikes.

I sat in Twin Pines' private library three days later, reading a book about models. Not that I thought reading about the things was much more exciting than building them, but I had to keep my cover image. Jesse Target liked models of all kinds, so that meant I built them *and* read books about them. I could think of worse ways to waste a day.

"Jesse?"

I slammed the model book shut, swung my legs back over the arm of the chair to sit upright, and looked up into bright blue eyes mirroring my own. "Ph-Philip Taylor," I stammered, getting to my feet. My lookalike stood before me, nervousness clearly written across his face. He looked good in blue jeans, a sky blue T-shirt, and black high-tops—but then, so did I.

How did he pick my outfit again? Does he have a camera in my room or something? He even wears his shirt untucked like me! I self-consciously straightened my shirt and ran a hand through my hair until I was as composed as him.

I know that in a library, you're supposed to be quiet, but the silence lingering between us only made us both more nervous. "Is your family here?" It was the first thing I could think of to break the silence.

He seemed relieved that I had spoken but shook his head. "No, I came by myself." He hesitated, then added, "To see you."

"Me?"

"Yes, I mean, you and I look alike, act alike, even *dress* alike. Not just halfway, but to the letter. I, I just had to see you a second time...." He bit his lower lip and drew a circle in the carpet with the toe of his shoe. "Does that make any sense to you?"

"Yes."

"Really? You understand it?"

I knew what he meant. I kind of wanted to see him again, too; I should have known he was the same way.

He looked up at me. "Have you been thinking about it?"

I blinked, honestly surprised. "You mean you have, too?"

"All the time. Weird, isn't it? We even *think* alike."

Better not be to the letter. If you tell me you're a private detective/ secret agent, I think I'll kill you.

I nodded. "Yeah, it is weird. Kind of makes you feel funny, doesn't it?"

"Yeah," he agreed.

There was silence again. This time, Philip broke it. "I know you don't really know me, and I don't know you, but since we do look alike and everything, I thought maybe we could get to know each other a bit. Maybe even be friends."

I wouldn't mind that at all—I could possibly find the answer to this mystery. I tried to tell myself that was the only reason I felt drawn to him but failed.

I shoved aside the tingly feeling I was getting all over just thinking about us being friends. "Sounds like a good idea to me," I replied.

"For real?"

"Sure. Why don't we go to the entertainment room, play some games, and get to know each other better?"

Philip's smile lit up his entire face, just like mine did when I really meant it. "Okay." We left the library, and I led the way to the huge entertainment room.

"Is that giant that wanted to beat me up still looking for you?" Philip asked as we passed a few kids who stopped and stared at us, whispering when we passed.

I ignored them and answered, "Yes, but there's nothing to worry about; he got it good for beating up another kid yesterday. He's under room arrest."

"What's that mean? Is it like house arrest?"

I smiled. "Just about."

The entertainment room was busy, as it normally was. Then we walked in.

I had never seen a place go so quiet so quickly. It was like a tidal wave. The kids sitting around the closest tables saw us, and conversation turned into staring at us. When the people at the table behind them noticed, they looked up and the same thing happened. This continued until the entire room was deadly silent and still. All the teens and adult supervisors stared at Philip and me standing in the doorway.

As Jesse Target, I was embarrassed with everyone staring at me, so I blushed, ducking my head. On my left, Philip did, too. *Great*, I thought hotly. *That mirror image movement sure didn't help us get away from this attention. If Philip's like Jesse Target, we both might stand here staring at the ground, drawing circles in the carpet with our toes for the rest of our lives.*

After a second, I felt a hand on my shoulder. Philip must have, too, because he also looked up.

Thank you, God, for sending Daisy to get us out of here. I silently praised as I looked up into her sharp green eyes.

She took over the situation in an instant. She raised her voice and said loudly enough so that the entire room could hear, "All right, everyone, go back to your games! You know Jesse, and most of you have seen Philip Taylor once. Go on, no need to stare like the world's flat and you're coming to its edge."

Daisy's humor and strong voice soon had everyone playing again. But as Daisy led us to a sheltered corner and got us a board game, I noticed we still got more than our fair share of glances. People spoke quieter, too, as though they were talking about us and didn't want us to hear.

After a while, Philip and I got a little more comfortable with each other. We stopped halting each time we looked at the other, and we could even laugh together. We used the game as an icebreaker. We talked about nothing serious, just "What's your favorite ice cream flavor?" and other stuff like that. We found out we had a lot in common, but by now, we weren't surprised.

We both liked chocolate chip mint ice cream; neither one of us had a girlfriend. Our favorite sport was basketball, with baseball a close second. He was allergic to milk, as was I, and we couldn't think of a food we loved better than hamburgers cooked outside on a grill.

By the time we finished the tenth game and Philip was shocked to look at his watch and find he was an hour late getting home, we knew a lot more about each other, and yet, nothing more than what we knew about ourselves.

I walked with Philip to the gate. "Thanks for coming, Philip. I honestly enjoyed talking and playing together."

He smiled back at me. "I enjoyed it, too. It's not often I can find a guy who is a real friend and not there just for the money my parents have."

I was flattered by his compliment but resisted the urge to duck my head. Instead, I asked, "Philip, may I ask you something?"

"Sure,"

"The first day we met, why were you alone with Smith? Why'd you leave the rest of your group?"

He shrugged. "I don t know. I guess I just wanted to meet one of the boys one-on-one and get to know him while I had the chance. I wanted to make a friend who was like you."

"Like me?"

"Yes. As I said, when you're rich, you have all the friends in the world, but only a very few are real friends. I figured here, I could find a boy who would be a real friend to me." He shrugged, looking bashful. "Sounds dumb, huh?"

I shook my head. "Not at all. Will you come back again? I want to show you my room."

He nodded, smiling in relief. "I'll come back as long as you'll have me around."

"Great."

Just as he was about to step out of the gate, he said, "We'll be friends for a long time, Jesse; I can tell."

I grinned back at him. "Me too."

7

SHADOW

Everyone was on top of me again the second I came back into the main building. They all wanted to know why Philip came back, what we talked about, and if we were going to be friends. I sidestepped answering most of the questions. If they knew Philip and I liked the same things, they'd be all over me to hit me up for things to impress the "rich kid."

Another question I doggedly avoided was if we were going to be friends. I wouldn't be able to hide it forever, but I wanted to as long as I could—the last thing I needed was dozens of "friends" all hanging out with me just to get in thick with Philip. Philip and I both didn't want or need that.

I found myself waiting enthusiastically for Philip's next visit; I couldn't wait to show him my room and see what he thought about it. I knew it would be nothing like his room. He was rich, and my room was just an orphan's, but somehow, I knew he would like it anyway.

Two afternoons after Philip's second visit, someone knocked on my door. When I opened it, there stood Philip. "Hey!" I cried excitedly. I was a bit surprised by my excitement at seeing him; not in all my life could I remember reacting like this to another person.

He grinned back at me. "Hi, Jesse."

Then we looked each other over and laughed. We were both wearing blue jeans, a red T-shirt, and white high-tops.

I took him by the shoulder and pulled him into my room, saying, "Come in here, Replica, before the guys realize you're not me and mob you."

Philip laughed as I closed the door. "Some guys actually came up to me to ask if I thought 'Philip' would come back and visit you soon." A look of concern replaced his smile. "I hope me coming hasn't been a drag on you."

"The guys?" He nodded. I shook my head. "They're not so bad; they're just excited about this whole thing, that's all."

"Oh." He shifted his feet, then asked with a puzzled look, "How do you think we keep doing it? Our clothes, I mean."

I shrugged. "I don t know." I sent him a mock suspicious look. "Haven't got a camera in my room, have you?"

He laughed but shook his head. "Nope, haven't got one in mine, have you?"

"Same here; I guess we just think alike."

"I thought we figured that out when we realized we both liked the same things." He looked around my room. His smile was genuine when he turned back to me and said, "I like your room."

"Thanks."

I invited him to sit on my bed, then plopped down facing him. We talked about models; he liked them just as much as Jesse Target did. The subject changed to movies and music. Again, we loved the same things.

After we chatted awhile, I asked him what his house looked like, and he began to describe a beautiful Victorian mansion. It was painted powder-blue, with darker blue shutters and trimmings. It was three stories high, with a wraparound porch, employee quarters, several bedroom suites, a huge library, a parlor, dining room, formal dining room, and a big kitchen, where you could always find a snack. The halls were wide and long—the doors all made of solid cedar wood—and marble fireplaces warmed every room—real ones that actually burned wood in the winter.

His dad had an office, his mom had a crafting room, and he had a room full of games of all kinds. There was also an indoor pool. There was even a creepy old attic, just like in the movies.

He then described the outside of the house; acres and acres of rolling green hills, valleys, and flat ground surrounded the estate. There were hundreds of flowers and gardens all over the place, with fountains, ponds, springs, and millions of little wildlife creatures.

Philip described a paradise, and I believed every word of it; something told me he didn't lie or exaggerate. When he finished, he leaned back and said, "It's a family estate. Been in my family for generations."

Over two weeks, our friendship grew more and more as Philip came to hang out with me at least three times a week. At first, the closeness between us scared us both; then we reasoned that since we were so much alike, of course we'd be close.

Even feeling what the other person was stopped being strange to us. In fact, it was kind of cool. I could tell when he was sad, and he could tell when I was, too, so then we could do something about it.

I saw the looks Ace and Daisy gave us but ignored them. I also ignored all the comments the others gave me. We were close friends; that was all.

The only worry I had was what would happen when I got another call to a case. I tensed each time a phone rang, afraid it might be for me and that when I answered it, I'd hear a familiar voice say, "Jesse Best," then give me an address and hang up.

Not that I liked my secret life any less now that Philip was around, but how could I explain disappearing to him? It was just like being adopted, except that I still lived at Twin Pines. I didn't like the idea of him knowing about the real me, no matter how close we were—it would put a big strain on him, and it could even put him in danger. Besides, I didn't think I'd ever quit my secret life; I'd die of boredom living as a civilian.

I simply had to find a solution that worked for the good of everyone before the next case.

A month after our first meeting, I stood by the gate, waiting for Philip, who was supposed to come by. He was ten minutes late—unusual for him; he was normally on time or early.

Maybe something came up spare of the moment, and he had to do that instead? I thought, turning away from the gate. I kicked a rock out of my way, shoving my hands into my pockets. I had really wanted to see him.

We hadn't been able to get together in over a week. There was something big he had to do in school, and I had been imprisoned, of sorts, to the Twin Pines grounds after being accused of something I hadn't done by a jerk jealous of my friendship with Philip. Today had been the first opportunity to get together, and it looked like it wasn't going to happen anyway.

"Jesse, wait up!"

I turned quickly, grinning widely. "Philip. I had just given up on you coming."

He laughed as he caught up to walk beside me. "No, I just took a different way today, so it took a little longer." He lowered his voice. "Can we go to your room and talk privately? I have to tell you something really important."

I didn't even have to look at him to see how serious he was; I could feel it. "Sure; just follow me." I ducked behind a hedge of bushes and began to lead him around the hordes of teens milling over the grounds. This was one of the ways I snuck out of Twin Pines when I got a call—I could sneak around everything and everyone, right up to my room.

Four minutes later, I closed the door behind us, locking it. Philip was already sitting on my bed, so I went to join him, then waited for him to begin.

He did so almost before I could sit down. "I don't think my parents trust me," he told me with a sour look. "They always have before, but I think they no longer do; something's changed."

I cocked my head to the side. "What made you come up with that conclusion so abruptly? Last time we met, you told me how close your family is."

He nodded, looking miserable. "I know; that's why this hurts so much." He put his elbows on his knees and rested his chin on his hands. "I think they put a shadow on me."

Now that surprised me. "On you?" I repeated unbelievingly. "Why?"

He sighed, shaking his head a little. "For the past couple of days, I've noticed these faces popping up much more than they should in my surroundings. Just today, I caught a car tailing me—that's what took so long getting here. I got a funny feeling and asked my chauffer to lose them."

"But why would your parents do that?"

"I haven't told them about you yet," he confessed, looking worried. "Don't take it wrong, Jesse, please—I'm not ashamed of you, it's just that, how can I tell my parents that I have a friend who may as well be me? They wouldn't understand it any more than we do."

"What do you tell them when you come over here?"

"I say, I'm going to hang out with my friends, and I'll be back in time for dinner. They give me permission, and then I leave. That's why I think they're having me shadowed; they must think I'm in some kind of trouble." He lifted his eyes to mine and pleaded, "Jesse, please believe me when I say I'm not ashamed of you. You're the best friend I've got. I'd never be ashamed of you. Do you believe me?"

"Yes." And I did. I could sympathize with him; his concerns brought the same anxiety I felt whenever I contemplated how to tell him about my disappearing.

His face brightened. "Really? You're not upset?"

"Of course not. But about this shadow—are you sure it's your parents?" A bad feeling had crept over me the minute I heard him say "shadow." It was probably the detective in me trying to push out, but I wanted to make sure everything was on the level without him knowing that's what I was doing.

He nodded, looking puzzled. "Sure, who else could it be?"

I shrugged then jokingly said, "Your parents have millions if you haven't noticed yet, Philip."

He looked shocked, worried, and scared all at the same time. Then he shoved my shoulder with a playful grin. "Get out of here! There's never been any trouble with the Taylor family in all the generations of wealth, and there have been dozens of kids."

"Just checking; I don't want to lose you. You're *my* best friend too." And he was.

"Thanks."

I grinned, but my mind was already drifting away to the search I would do that night. Philip had pushed off the idea of a stalker or kidnapper, but I wouldn't. I had worked too many cases where the child had been stalked and then kidnapped to let this go without at least doing a preliminary search.

"Listen, why don't you and I come up with something you can tell your parents when you get home tonight?" I suggested.

"It's not right to worry them, and then your shadow would stop harassing you. I'm sure we can think of something if we do it together."

He brightened. "Okay, but we can't spend all afternoon on it—I want us to have *some* fun, at least."

Laughing, I agreed.

8

THE MEDALLION

"So, what happened?" I asked, leaning forward eagerly.

Philip was trying hard to keep from laughing as he continued his tale, "Well, Allis was fighting the swordfish with all his might when Steve jumped up, so excited he couldn't stay seated any longer. Allis had just reeled it in enough so that we could see it fighting to get away when Steve smashed Allis on the shoulder. It was completely innocent—Steve's kind of an airhead. Well, anyway, Steve slapped him just when he was leaning forward to get more power. *Wham!* Allis lost his balance, tumbled overboard, and the swordfish towed him all over the place, screaming at the top of his lungs for us to get him, but too stubborn to let go!"

The image of Allis Billson being towed through the water by the biggest swordfish any of the young fishermen had ever seen struck me as hilarious. I fell backward on my bed, laughing as Philip finally let his laughter out to mingle pleasantly with mine.

We had been swapping stories about our lives ever since finishing the letter Philip would read to his parents that night at dinner. It was simply worded, explaining about us, how we met, what good friends we had become, and that both of us were born-again Christians, so there was nothing for them to worry about. We even included a picture of us standing together under one of the huge pine trees at the front of the building. Philip and I were convinced it was enough to set any parents' mind at ease, and if not, Philip was going to offer to bring them here to meet me.

"I wish you'd been there, Jesse. It was so funny! It got even better when all of us were laughing too hard to do anything," Philip said, laughing even more.

"Did Allis ever get the fish?" I asked, linking my fingers behind my head and looking up at the ceiling.

"No, it broke the line and got away; we've gone fishing there a lot ever since. Allis is determined to get that fish and have it mounted. We've seen it a few times, but I think it's smart enough now not to eat fish on hooks."

I chuckled but remained lying as Philip sat up, wiping tears from his eyes. "That must have been fun," I said after a minute. What I wasn't telling him was that I had gone shark fishing in Hawaii three years ago. I had been on a case working with my dad at the time. The tale behind the shark tooth necklace I had stashed away with my other Jesse Best things was quite interesting. Of course, I'd never be able to tell him about it.

"It was." Philip's face lit up. "Hey, do you think I can get Twin Pines to let you come next time? I don't think the guys would mind having one more along," he grinned. "I think they'd go crazy trying to tell which one of us is Philip and which one is Jesse."

I laughed. "Philip, your family is the leading donors—you could ask the superintendent if all the teens can go, and he'd agree!"

"Well, then, you better be ready to go swordfish fishing 'cause next time we head out, I'm swinging by here to pick you up first."

"Thanks."

We were quiet for a minute as we thought about what that fishing trip might be like. I smiled as I thought how astonished his friends would be to find that Philip had a double.

Another thought, this one disturbing, crept into my mind. Would they even accept me? In the knowing world's eyes, I was just a penniless orphan, and they were all millionaires. I'd just have to wait and find out, then go with it.

"Hey, I didn't know you wore a necklace," Philip noted, breaking into my thoughts.

I looked up at him and nodded. Sitting up, I pulled on the sturdy gold chain I always wore around my neck. A gold emblem the size of a silver dollar popped out from under my shirt. A magnificent dove's head rose from the bottom and into the center. Cleverly etched in the feathering of the dove's neck was a tiny, empty cross, with two swords clashed on the left side. Two flags lay on the right side, crossed by their flagpoles and fluttering in the wind. One was the American flag, the other the Christian. Bordering the top-half of the round disc was strange writing. I had no idea what it said and probably never would.

I fingered the medallion affectionately. "My parents put this around my neck when I was a year old. The same doctor who performed the C-section on Mom gave it to them for me. I don't know why he went to the trouble of having something so elaborate made for a one-year-old he only saw three times in his life— two of those times yet to happen as of then.

"I don't remember it, but Mom and Dad told me dozens of times about the day Dr. Marlow came to give this to them. He knocked on our door the day before my birthday and told my parents he had a gift for me; he wanted me to have it always." I frowned, puzzled by the last part of his message. "He told them to tell me when I got older and could understand that I should never take the medallion off, not even for a second. He said if anything ever happened to Dad and Mom, this medallion would provide me a sure future." I shrugged. "I don't know why he thought that. Sure, it's pure gold and expertly crafted, but it would never get more than around twelve thousand dollars if I sold it—nothing to ensure me a future."

Letting the medallion drop to rest against my chest, I looked up. "Philip?" I questioned, reaching out to shake him. "Philip, are you all right? You look like you're in some kind of trance."

He blinked and licked dry lips before looking up at me. His face was pale. "You don't know what that is?" he whispered, pointing to my necklace.

I shook my head slowly. "No. Maybe the writing on the top is a clue, but I haven't been able to figure it out or find someone who knows it. Why? Do you know what it is?"

He nodded, licking his lips again.

I waited, but he said nothing. "Philip, what is it..." my words trailed off as I noticed, for the first time, a gold chain also hung around Philip's neck, disappearing beneath his shirt. My eyes grew wide. I looked at him, shaking my head. "No. No way—it's impossible!"

He shook his head mutely, reaching for my necklace.

I reached out too, pinching the sturdy chain between my thumb and forefinger. With trembling hands, I gently pulled the necklace he wore into view. I was staring at the same medallion Dr. Marlow had given my parents to put on me.

9

SEVERED

We looked at each other, back at the identical medallions, then back at each other. Neither of us spoke for several minutes.

Finally, I was able to swallow around the basketball-sized lump wedged into my throat and whispered, "It's true. They were right—we *are* twins."

Philip shook his head, sounding sick as he denied, "No, we can't be. We were in two different families, from two different worlds. We can't be twins. We just can't be!"

"You think I want us to be twins?" I demanded, feeling just as sick as he looked. "I know we grew up in two different families. I know we grew up in two different worlds—but how else can you explain all this?

"I've tried, Philip. Man, how I've tried! Ever since meeting you, I tried thinking of some other explanation—I even convinced myself it was just a coincidence! But there are just too many things we have in common! We're identical twins. Even if we tossed out our likeness, sensing each other's feelings, how it's getting stronger the more time we spend with each other, and everything else, we can't toss out the fact that we're both wearing the same exact medallion around our necks."

He sat there a minute, absorbing my tirade of words. Then he looked at me and said, "You're a Taylor."

"No!" I shouted. "You're a Target!"

He glared at me. "No, I'm not! I'm not the one wearing the Taylor Crest—that's what that is, Jesse! It's the Taylor Crest, created by the first-ever Taylor and only worn by Taylors. That's why Dr. Marlow told your parents it would ensure you a future. If you found out what it was and came to my estate, it'd be obvious in a second that we're twins, and you'd become a millionaire in a matter of hours! It's *you* who's been lied to all his life."

Even a detective/secret agent can get so mad he can't see; that's what happened to me. I needed someone to vent my churning emotions on, and when Philip dared to say my parents lied to me, I dove at him.

And so our first fight began. We pushed and shoved each other across the bed, then crashed to the floor. We rolled left to right to left again, punching, yelling, and screaming, letting out on the other all the emotions that churned inside us, even though it was really neither of our faults.

Suddenly, a strong arm circled around my neck. I let go of Philip's shirt to grab the limb that was strangling me as it forced me away from Philip. At the same time, another arm circled Philip's neck, pulling him away from me. Ace held us both as far apart as he could and ordered us to stop trying to squirm loose and get at each other.

Finally, we calmed down enough that he could let go of our necks and take a fistful of our T-shirts instead. Stern-looking, he demanded, "What's this all about? You two have been good friends over the past few weeks, and now I come in to find you trying to bash the other's brains out."

"It's his fault!" We both accused, pointing at the other.

"Why didn't I see that coming?" Ace asked, rolling his eyes toward the ceiling. Looking at both of us, he said, "Why don't you tell me what's going on? One at a time."

Naturally, we both talked at the same time. Philip said, "He's a Taylor, but he won't accept it!" While I said, "He's a Target, but he refuses to believe it!"

"Boys, this is getting us nowhere. Jesse, give me one sentence, then Philip, you give me one."

I drew in a deep breath and babbled, "We were sitting here, just chilling out when he saw my necklace and I took it out and told him how I got it, then I looked up and saw he was looking weird, and I saw we were wearing the same medallions, then he said I was a Taylor—but it's not true, Mr. Ace, you know it's not true!" Looking back, I was glad I'd remembered to add the "mister" before his name.

Ace shook his head. "Jesse, that's the worst run-on sentence I've ever heard."

Philip spoke up, anxious to have his turn. "He's a Taylor as sure as I am! Look at our medallions—they're identical." He looked up at Ace. "You know what this medallion is? It's the Taylor Crest, and only Taylors wear it. What's that tell you, sir? That he's a Taylor, not a Target, just like I said. He's got to be stupid not to agree."

"Stupid, am I?" I bellowed. "You're the stupid one! The Taylors adopted you; it's *your* parents who are the liars!"

He lunged at me, but Ace held us both steady as Philip shouted, "You're the liar! Why would you be wearing the Taylor Crest if I were the one in the wrong home?"

"Well, then, you can have it!" I screamed, whipping it over my head and shoving it into his hands. "You can have your Ritzy mansion, your fancy limo and family jet. You can have all your millions upon billions of dollars and your lying parents! I don't want any of it! I don't care if I never see you again!"

Clutching my ex-medallion to his chest, Philip spit out, "Fine! I couldn't care less if I never saw you again, either!" He wrenched away from Ace's grip and ran out the door.

I also pulled out of Ace's grip and ran to the door, shouting, "Don't ever come back!" Breathing hard, I slammed the door as hard as I could, nearly cracking it.

Ace cleared his throat to remind me he was still there.

I looked up and glared at him. "Don't say a word, Ace. Not a word." I stomped over to my bed and plopped down. I saw the pillow Philip had been leaning up against and snatched it, throwing it across the room. I didn't want anything he'd touched near me.

Ace spoke to me, "Jesse—"

"Not a word, Ace!" I yelled, as close to being out of control as I'd come since my parents' deaths. "Just get out."

Wordlessly, he walked over and opened the door. Before he left, he said, "If you need us—"

"Out, Ace!"

He left, closing the door behind him.

10

GETTING BACK ON MY FEET

I stayed locked inside my room for two days. I wouldn't let any-one in, not even Ace and Daisy. I even went as far as to barri-cade the door, just to be sure no one could get in.

I replayed everything that had happened since meeting Philip over and over in my head. Then I went even further back and replayed my whole life, trying to figure out how my life was sud-denly falling apart.

It just didn't make any sense. My mom had been pregnant al-most full-term, then she'd had a C-section, and I was born. They brought me home, and I lived with them. There was absolutely no way I could have been a Taylor and mysteriously gotten into the Targets' home. Even if someone had lied to me about it, ev-eryone assured me the story I knew as my own was true. I wasn't adopted. So how could I explain what was soon becoming a very ugly, very dirty, truth?

Then there were the other questions, like why the Taylors would give me up for adoption in the first place if it were true.

Philip had told me that he'd been born by C-section, too (and like an idiot, I hadn't let myself see the twin thing coming), but his mom had run into complications, and she wouldn't ever be able to have another baby. Philip had told me how much his parents had wanted children—no less than four. So why had they given up a child that would have at least given them half the number they really wanted? Especially when I had been a twin?

An awful thought hit me, settling in my stomach like a gulp of sour milk. Had there been something wrong with me, so they hadn't wanted to keep me? But that couldn't be right because there was nothing wrong with me. And since Philip and I shared everything, wouldn't whatever had allegedly been wrong with me been wrong with him, too? It just didn't make sense.

None of it did.

By the night of the second day, I knew I had some very important things to do and hard things to face. I un-barricaded my door and slipped into the hall, glad no one was there to see me; I didn't want to have to talk to anyone. I wasn't sure if everyone knew about the medallions and what that implied or not, but I really didn't want to have to deal with them either way.

I slipped down to the end of the hall, where Ace and Daisy's apartment was. Lifting my hand, I knocked slowly. The door opened, and Daisy stood there, smiling compassionately and reaching out a hand to me. I walked into her arms and allowed her to hold me for several minutes before pulling away.

Ace was there, too, sitting on the couch. He motioned for me to take the armchair, where kids sat when they came to them as Floor Parents to help them work out problems. As I sat, Daisy did too on the couch next to Ace so they could both see me, watch me.

We were silent for a long time before I started to speak. "I'm sorry. I'm sorry for how I've been acting these past two days."

They both nodded, accepting my apology and forgiving my behavior. Ace reached out and squeezed my shoulder while Daisy asked softly, "Are you all right?"

I shook my head. I looked up at them and offered a broken, beaten smile. "But I'm okay."

"You had us worried."

I knew exactly what they were talking about. When my parents died, I freaked out for a few weeks. I closed myself off from everyone, determined to deal with the pain by myself instead of letting anyone comfort me. Though I'd been tempted to do the same thing this time, I'd learned from that experience that shutting out the world wasn't the way to deal.

"You didn't tell the director, did you?" If they told the CIA director I'd shut myself away again, it might have cost me that part of my secret life; unstable people weren't allowed in active duty.

They shook their heads. "We wanted to give you a chance to come to us," Daisy said.

I smiled at them gratefully. "Thank you; you saved my career."

"It's a career worth saving."

I sighed, closing my eyes and leaning back against the chair. "I still want to rebel against it, but I know you were right about Philip and me being identical twins." I looked at them, the helplessness again washing over me. "But how? How is this possible?"

"I wish we could tell you, Jesse," Ace lamented. "But it's come as a shock to all of us. Until meeting Philip Taylor, I would have sworn you were a born-and-blood Target."

I dropped my head. "I...I think I'm going to have to call Philip. We've got to talk." I looked back at them. "Whatever happened, it wasn't fair that we were separated—not identical twins. I want to find out who's responsible for this and why it happened. Nothing I can think of makes any sense, not when all the facts are put into the picture. Maybe there's something we don't know." I laughed at myself. "Yeah, there must be a *lot* of things we don't know. But one will unravel this whole mess."

They nodded, agreeing that I'd chosen a good starting point. I glanced at my watch. "It's too late to call him now, so I'll do it tomorrow." I stopped. "Do I have to go to school?"

The pair exchanged one of those husband-wife looks, then shook their heads. "You've been out for two days—one more won't hurt, just to get your head clear."

"Thanks."

11
FUSING

I passed my cell phone from one hand to the other, trying to work up enough nerve to call. After our parting words, I wasn't even sure he'd listen to me. It was funny; I'd faced street thugs, murderers, and terrorists without a nerve popping up, but when it came to making a simple phone call, I suddenly had no guts. Finally, I managed to punch in the numbers—quickly, so I couldn't lose my nerve.

Lifting the phone to my ear, I found myself praying, *Please, Lord, let him at least hear me out. I have to know. I can't live the rest of my life wondering. Please help us. Both of us.*

Maybe you think it's weird I would pray—me, a detective/secret agent. But I pray all the time, and never so much as when I'm on a case or mission. I mean, without God, how was I supposed to face the danger of fighting crime? Terrorists aren't exactly the nicest people to the agents they capture; I couldn't do it without faith in God.

The call went through.

"Hello?" Philip's questioning voice asked. He wouldn't have recognized the number on his screen, as I had never called with my cell phone before—I don't think he even knew I had one.

"Um, Philip? It's me, Jesse."

"What do you want?" No warmth, but at least he wasn't hanging up yet.

"I have to talk to you. *We've* got to talk. Will you come over? Please?"

There was a long, agonizing silence, then, "I have to do my homework first, but I'll be over around five."

"Perfect. Thanks for coming *and* for not hanging up."

"I probably should have." Was that a glimmer of humor? "I have to go, Jesse—I've got a ton of homework before I can come over."

"I'll be waiting."

We both hung up at the same time. Of course.

A half-hour after five, I nearly gave up waiting. But then, a knock—hesitant, sounded against my door. I opened it quickly. The shock of seeing myself in Philip came as an unpleasant sensation. Even our senses seemed to realize something had gone wrong between us.

"Come in," I invited, feeling stiff, formal.

As he came in, he looked just as stiff as I felt.

We sat on the bed, facing each other as we had that day—one that seemed like millenniums away now. There was silence, uncomfortable silence, for several minutes.

Finally, I drew in a deep breath. "Do you want me to apologize?"

"Will you?"

A slow grin spread across my face. I shook my head. "No."

A slow grin spread across his face, too. "Good, because I won't, either."

I nodded, accepting his words.

Again, there was silence.

Again, I broke it. "I don't see how it's possible. Me being what you said I was."

"It's not exactly a dirty word, you know."

I looked up at him. He was grinning our slow, lazy grin again. "Yeah, I know, but try calling yourself a Target."

His grin grew bigger. "No can do."

I grinned back at him. "Yeah, that's what I thought. So, anyway, I think we have to talk about it."

"Okay. What's there to say?" Without letting me answer, he went on, anger heating his words. "That something really weird happened? That someone, maybe a lot of someones, lied to both of us? That we were unfairly separated too young to remember the other, except for an unfillable ache?—"

"Wait a second!" I cut in. "You feel it, too?" All my life, I'd felt lonely for someone. Even when I was with my parents or friends, I would feel this unexplainable ache deep inside, like part of me was missing. It was something I'd never told anyone.

Philip nodded. "I feel it. It's been slowly filling in since I started hanging around you."

It was my turn to nod. Now that he mentioned it, I did feel something had started to replace the emptiness. "You also feel how I do about our situation?"

"How else am I to feel? And I don't mean because we share feelings."

I nodded agreement. "So, tell me how you think it happened."

He shook his head. "No, you'll punch me again."

I frowned. "You think it was my parents' fault?"

"I told you that my parents wanted more children. Why would they give up the one they had?"

I clenched my fists. "Well, why don't you think of your parents as the bad guys for once? Maybe they thought something was wrong with me, so they dumped me."

He clenched his fists, too. "Oh yeah? Well, maybe your parents were so desperate for a kid that they came in and stole you!"

I was just about to lay into him again when I remembered my breathing trick. Quickly, I started controlling my breaths. Beside me, Philip was slowly counting to ten under his breath.

We looked up at each other, shook our heads, and grinned.

"Getting mad at each other isn't going to do anything for us," we both said together, then laughed. It felt so good to laugh with him again.

"Okay," I said, "let me tell you why this is so weird on my side."

Philip nodded. "Okay. Then I'll tell you my side."

I nodded and began. I told him everything about Mom's pregnancy and the C-section. I told him how everyone I ever met guaranteed I was the same baby that the Targets brought home from the hospital; there was no bizarre switch during the years. I grew up in the Targets' home. I was their child, no questions asked.

When I had finished, Philip nodded, looking stumped. "Yeah, my story's about the same. So, how did it happen?" He looked at me, anguish in his eyes. "Do you think we've been lied to all our lives?"

I shook my head. "I don't know, Philip. My parents never lied to me—ever."

"Neither have mine."

"So, how did this whole mess happen?"

Neither of us had an answer.

Then suddenly, an idea popped into my head. It was so shocking that I nearly tumbled off the bed. Reaching out, I grabbed Philip's shirt and demanded, "Philip, what if we are *both* adopted?"

He stared at me. "What?"

"What if neither of us is a Taylor or a Target? What if our moms lost their previous babies due to complications, then adopted babies to fill that void? I know my mom was in the hospital a couple of weeks. If they rushed it, they could have found me and adopted me during that time. What about you?"

He nodded slowly. "We stayed in the hospital a couple of weeks, too. They could have adopted me." He looked up at me. "But that's horrible, isn't it? That they adopted us then never told us. I wouldn't have cared—I'd rather have been told than to have found out like this."

"Hey, there's still no proof that we are both adopted," I said, reneging on the idea.

"No, but isn't it better than any of your other ideas? I know it is about mine."

I nodded. "Yeah, I guess it is. But at the same time, it's not—not for one of our parents."

"Why this time?"

"Well, someone didn't adopt us both. Twins shouldn't be separated, agreed?"

"Agreed, but what if neither of them knew about us?"

I frowned. "How could they not?"

"What if our birth mom put us in two different orphanages? What if it's her fault that we were separated? Then none of our parents are the bad guys."

"I guess so."

"But, like you said, we may not even be adopted." He looked glum again.

I thought about it. "Well, there's one way we can tell for sure."

"What is it? Ask?"

"No, not yet—I thought we could get a DNA test."

"We're just a couple of teenagers—how are we going to get something like that done without telling the adults?"

I bit my lower lip. *If we were just two normal kids, it'd be tough. But I'm not normal. I'm a detective/secret agent and have contacts that will get it done for us.* "I might have a way we can do it," I said carefully, "but it would take a little while."

He shrugged. "We haven't known for fourteen years; what're a few weeks compared to that? What do we do?"

"You'll have to get a DNA sample from your parents without letting them know what you're doing—something like hair. After you get that, each of us will provide DNA samples to be cross-referenced with theirs. I'll talk to this person I know and see if she'll help us or not, then we'll know for sure."

Philip was silent a long moment before asking softly, "What if we weren't adopted? Your medallion—"

"I can't think about that right now, Philip," I cut in quickly. "Let's just wait for the DNA test to settle it. We can deal with my medallion later, okay?"

He nodded slowly. "Okay."

I could sense his doubt, and I drew in a deep breath against the feelings welling up inside me. I was afraid he was thinking the same thing I was, and I was desperately hoping we were both wrong. Impulsively, I blurted out, "Hey, Philip, promise me something."

He cocked his head in question.

I drew in another deep breath and worded a disclaimer I didn't want to make. "If things get crazy, promise me you won't think I set this up to get your fortune?"

He wrinkled his forehead. "What do you mean?"

"I'm holding on to the fact this DNA test will prove we were both adopted, but if it doesn't ..." I swallowed hard on the option my mind was trying to force me to consider. "If things get crazy, don't ever believe anyone who says I wanted it this way. I may be just an orphan, living in a home for teenagers with no place to go, but I would rather have that and my parents than all your fortune without them."

He looked at me for a long minute before reaching out and squeezing my shoulder. "Jesse, if things get crazy, just *let* some jerk try to accuse you of gold-digging—he won't do it twice."

We were silent a long time before I spoke again. "No matter what happens, I still want us to be friends. These last couple of days, when we were mad at each other, were terrible. I missed you, and I don't want to lose you again."

He smiled. "Yeah, same for me. No matter what these results say, let's never let anything drive us apart."

"Deal."

12
RESULTS

I woke up sometime late next Monday night to a gentle shake of my shoulders. I rolled over, opening my eyes. "Daisy, Ace. What's up?" I raised myself on my elbows and turned to face the older couple.

"We knew you'd want them the minute they came." Daisy held out an envelope to me.

I cocked an eyebrow. "The results?"

Daisy's head bobbed rapidly. "Yes. We haven't even looked at them; we wanted you to be the first."

My first instinct was to grab the envelope out of her hands and rip it open, but I followed my second. I clasped my hands behind my back. "I don't want to see them until Philip can see them with me. I decided that yesterday. If the results came when he couldn't be here with me to see them for the first time, I'd wait until he could get here. You can look at them if you want, but I'm not until morning."

Ace shook his head. "No. We want you and Philip to be the first. We'll practice patience and wait until you look at them."

Daisy nodded and began to set them on my desk, but I stopped her. "Will you please bring them back to your room with you?" I grinned sheepishly. "I don't know if I can trust myself to wait if they're here."

Daisy nodded and tucked the envelope into her bag. "We'll leave so you can go back to sleep—you have an algebra test tomorrow, and you'll need your rest." She sounded very much like the Floor Mom instead of an ex-agent when she said that.

I leaned back and burrowed under the light blanket. "I can hardly wait," I grumbled. I hated algebra, even if I didn't have trouble with it like lots of other teens. There was just something about it that came across to me as a waste of time and life. Who cared if you took any letter from the alphabet and called it a five?

Daisy laughed while Ace ruffled my hair. "Good night, Jesse. I hope you can sleep after the news."

I smiled up at them as they turned to leave. "I've slept after hearing other bits of important news. I guess I'll sleep tonight."

The next morning I woke up with a bound. I got ready super fast—I guess I figured if I was moving faster than normal, so would everything else. Hah, so wrong. Getting ready fast just left me with extra empty time on my hands.

While I waited for time to crawl by so I could leave to eat breakfast with the rest of the teens, I decided to pick up my Bible and memorize a few more verses—a habit my parents grained into me since I was little. They taught me two things—one, how to be a good detective/agent, and two, to love, honor, and respect God all my life. One way to show my love for God was to study and memorize His Word; it had come in handy when I was undercover on a mission and couldn't bring my Bible along.

I had thoroughly memorized one verse in 1 Corinthians, chapter 13, and was working on a second when I heard the first sounds of life in the hallway. I waited for the flow to increase to more than a tiny trickle before placing my bookmark in the passage and getting up to join them.

It was Ace's idea not to be the first one out in the morning or the last one out at night. He said the more average I was, the less suspicious I would be. I joined the flow of "mediocre" teens and followed them to the cafeteria.

I had never eaten such a blah meal in my life. I was sure the food was great because everyone else complimented it, but to me, it was tasteless and dry; my taste buds must have shot to the future with the rest of my senses. All through school hours, I was only there in body. However, in mind and spirit, I was in my room with Philip opening an envelope that could change both our lives forever.

The first sense I used all day was hearing when I listened as the bell rang to announce classes were over. I was the first one out of the mathematics classroom and down the hall.

I broke the rule of always being neat by hazardously tossing my book bag onto the bed. I grabbed my cellphone from where I kept it hidden in a slot we'd built in the underside frame of my bed.

I dialed Philip's number without thinking and placed the phone to my ear. It rang once, twice, three times, and it wasn't picked up. *Come on, Philip, answer me,* I thought, tapping my foot and checking my watch. School was out, but he might be in the middle of gathering books and making plans with friends and stuff.

Tactless, Jesse Best! I scolded as I hung up to call back later. *You are trained to be able to control all kinds of situations like a pro. This certainly isn't how a pro would handle it. Call back in an hour and speak in a controlled, unemotional tone.*

I nodded to myself in satisfaction. It was probably a good thing he hadn't answered; I'd have gushed out the news and would have had to repeat it a dozen times before he got it. By not answering, he gave me the time I needed to compose myself.

An hour later, I picked up my cell again. Keeping myself under strong control, I slowly punched in the numbers. I raised the phone to my ear, and when Philip picked up, I spoke in a distinguished but normal voice, "Hey, Philip, it's Jesse. What are you doing right now?"

"Nothing—homework."

I smiled. "Nothing or homework?"

"Homework *is* nothing when it's dumb."

"Not quite, but close enough."

"Have a better alternative than homework?" He asked hopefully.

"I might. Can you guess what just came in?"

There was a long pause before a whisper, "The results?"

"Yes."

"Were we?"

"I haven't let myself open them yet to see. I want us to look together."

"I'm coming right now."

"What about your homework?"

"Jesse, this is huge! I can do boring homework anytime."

"See you in twenty minutes."

"Make that ten." In the background, I heard a door slam.

"Philip, no speeding." I admonished firmly. "Get here in twenty minutes, and not a second sooner. Keeping the law comes before finding out. Promise?"

He sighed heavily. "Sure, I promise."

"I'm hanging up. Come straight to my room when you get here."

Exactly twenty minutes later, Philip came into my room. We had stopped the rule of knocking before entering during the second week of our friendship. One, we were wearing out my door, and two, it alerted the guys that it wasn't me. Who knocked on his own door?

"Where is it?" He panted.

I surveyed him while shutting the door he had left open. It looked like he'd run up the flights of stairs and barely paused to open the door before charging in. "Take two seconds to regain your breath, and I'll tell you," I told him, sitting on the foot of my bed and letting him take the head.

He drew in several deep breaths. "Well?" He demanded.

I leaned back and slipped the envelope from under my bed. Philip bounced down to my side of the bed and nearly sat on top of me to see.

Slowly, I cracked the seal on the envelope and pulled out a single piece of paper. We leaned closer together as we both read through the words. My heart began racing, and I lowered the sheet to my lap.

Philip watched me draw in several deep breaths. He said nothing as I processed the news we'd both already known, but I hadn't wanted to believe. After several moments, he gave my shoulder a tight squeeze and promised, "We'll find the truth, Jesse. Nobody knows why you didn't grow up with me. We shouldn't assume anything."

I nodded, but it took me a few swallows before I loosened my vocal cords enough to speak. "They didn't do anything wrong, Philip. I know my parents. I don't know what happened, but I know they couldn't have kidnapped me from you guys."

He shook his head. "That was just some crazy idea I had when I was mad. I shouldn't have ever mentioned it."

I shook my head. "I don't blame you. As you said, we'll find the truth." I looked over at him, determination descending firmly upon me. "We have to talk to your parents—they're the only ones who can tell us why we grew up separated and how I got in the Targets' family."

He nodded gravely. I think both of us were aware that the secrets surrounding our past were far from being over and that neither of our parents was fully cleared from being smeared.

He gave me a concerned look. "You going to be okay?"

I shrugged. "I don't know yet. I don't feel like a Taylor." The fact was I felt nothing. I guess I had numbed myself so I couldn't feel anything. Time would take its toll, and I'd soon deal with the news I'd just learned.

He seemed to get it. "When you need to talk, you can call me. I know if things had been different, you'd say the same to me."

I nodded my head, grateful that he understood what I was feeling and he would support me.

13
IT BEGINS

We decided to wait a couple of days before taking the DNA results to Philip's parents and asking them about it. We really didn't voice a reason, but I think Philip guessed I needed the time to process my new family tree before facing more unexpected things from my past. Getting permission for me to leave the grounds was very simple, with Philip Taylor at my side. Mr. Hoffman was glad to permit one of his wards to go to a rich donor's house for the evening. The glance he gave me when we were leaving warned me to behave. I smiled reassuringly at him and nodded.

"I can't wait to see Wade's face when we both come around the corner," Philip gleefully said as we left Twin Pines through the big gate.

I looked at Philip. "You're going to enjoy this, aren't you?"

He looked a little sheepish. I think he felt guilty for his reaction because he knew I was still dealing with the knowledge I wasn't who I thought I was. "Part of it, yes," he admitted. "I'm not going to enjoy whatever my parents tell us, but I am going to enjoy watching people's expressions as they see us together for the first time. Do you think you will?"

"I'm too nervous to enjoy anything!" I complained. Truthfully, I wasn't overly nervous. I had faced the facts, and now I wanted answers, but Jesse Target would be nervous about the coming event. "I can't understand what happened to me! We're just going to meet two people." I sighed and looked at the sky. "Two very rich, accomplished, elegant, sophisticated, way outside my lower class, people."

Philip grinned knowingly. "You don't have to be nervous; my parents are just like me. None of us are stuck up. You don't have to be afraid or feel intimidated by them—they're just people."

I nodded, shrugging restlessly. "I know. It's just that I feel like they won't accept me because I don't have a fortune." I held up my hand to stop his protests. "I know, you just told me it doesn't matter, but I still feel inadequate." And I did—as Jesse Target. Jesse Best was as cool as ever and eager for clues to chase that would solve the mystery concerning my family situation.

Philip put his hand on my shoulder. "You, Jesse Target, will never be 'inadequate,' no matter what—and I'm not just saying that, either. I really believe there's nothing you can't do."

I was silent as we walked around the corner. I glanced at him out of the corner of my eye. Was he twin worshiping me, or was he receiving Jesse Best signals as well as Jesse Target?

That was a chilling thought. I could control almost everything that might give me away, but how was I supposed to control something even scientists couldn't figure out? I'd just have to keep my eye on it.

The door on the driver's side of the huge, powder blue limo opened, and out stepped the man I knew from Philip's descriptions as Wade White.

"Hello, Master Philip—" He stopped short when he looked up and saw us standing side by side, hands in our pockets. "Wha...?"

We looked at each other and grinned mischievously; maybe I *was* going to enjoy this part. "Hello, Mr. Wade, I hope you didn't get bored waiting here for me," we said together.

The ordinarily sophisticated and well-composed chauffer was now quite different in manner and attire. He stared at us, shoulders stooped, mouth slightly opened, having nothing to say.

Philip laughed. "This is the friend I told you about. He's coming home to meet my parents tonight." He added, after a moment's thought, "He could be my identical twin, couldn't he?"

We both watched closely for any reaction. If the staff knew anything at all about me, there was a good chance this old man would—he had been around for years at the Taylor estate.

But Wade didn't react like he'd known of me. He straightened and composed himself. "Nice to meet you, young sir. Shall I open the door, Master Philip?" he said with great dignity.

Philip was equally dignified when he nodded, then led the way into the back seat.

As Jesse Best, I had ridden in limos before, but Jesse Target never had. I looked around the spacious interior with wide eyes and an open mouth. I touched and felt everything, murmuring in awe as I did.

Philip sat in his favorite seat by the left-side window, watching with pleasure. "You like it?" He asked when I came to sit on the seat beside him.

I looked around again before finding my voice. "Like it? It's awesome! You could live in here and never have to leave!"

"Wrong on two counts." He ticked them off on his fingers. "There's not enough food to never leave, and there's no bathroom in here."

I shrugged. "Well, then, you could basically live in here." Philip agreed with that.

As we drove along, he showed me what all the gizmos and gadgets did. It was a pretty impressive rig, even to Jesse Best.

"Philip, is that car the one that's been following you?" I asked after a fifteen-minute drive from Twin Pines. I had noticed it following us ten minutes ago. I wondered if it was the same shadow or if we were being shadowed because I was in the car.

Philip turned in his seat to see out the back window. He turned around a moment later. "Yes, that's the car—I know because the windows are tinted too dark to see in. I'd think it'd be illegal to have them tinted so dark—it's got to be hard to see out. Might cause an accident."

"Might," I agreed.

For the rest of the time, I watched the car. It was good—it never allowed us to get close to it. It kept us separated by three cars all the time. If one car pulled out, it'd hang back until another took its place. Anyone who happened to be watching would never have noticed it was tailing us.

Philip suddenly grabbed my arm. I jerked my head around to look at him, wondering if something was wrong.

He was pointing out his window. "There it is. *Blessed Rest.*"

I turned and followed his finger with my eyes. Perched high on a grassy knoll several acres into a rolling estate of rich beauty stood a three-story Victorian mansion. "Oh, Philip," I murmured. I didn't have to pretend to be awed by it—the Taylor family estate was magnificent. Everything he had told me had been true, only much more glorious in person than in words.

"Awesome, isn't it? The prettiest estate you've ever seen?"

I nodded and swung around to watch as the huge white iron gates with pale blue tips slid closed. I also saw our shadow drive past and keep going. Then I turned back around to watch our approach up the winding driveway, hedged in by manicured bushes and flowers.

"Now I know what Cinderella must have felt like when arriving at the palace," I told Philip as we stopped in front of the marble steps leading up to a huge double door.

A man in a pale blue waistcoat and white dress pants stepped forward and opened the door facing the steps.

Philip got out first and stopped the valet when he tried to close the door before I got out. "Just a minute, Whittaker—I brought a friend home with me. He's going to meet my parents."

"Oh, forgive me, Master Philip!" He said and pulled the door wide open. I stepped out. "Why, Master Philip!" Whittaker exclaimed, staring at me in astonishment. "He looks just like you!"

"You might even say we're replicas," Philip agreed, then turned to me. "Come on, let's go."

As he walked beside me up the steps, he whispered, "I want to get to the library before news of what you look like gets to my parents. In a household like mine, news like this will travel faster than soppy ice cream can melt at a July picnic."

I stopped dead still when the doors were opened inward by a grinning, young butler. It wasn't the nonstandard butler that stopped me in my tracks; it was the incredible entryway I walked into.

"This room is bigger than the cafeteria back at Twin Pines!" I gasped, turning in circles to see everything. *Blessed Rest* was doing a good job of keeping Jesse Target gapping.

The room was at least 50 feet by 75. The ceiling had to go all the way up to the attic, and right in the center of it hung a glorious crystal chandelier with hundreds of tiny lights that shone like fireflies. The walls were decorated with art—good art, not the modern art of this age. It was old art; I guessed some of the paintings went back several generations. The floor was covered in rich, glossy tiles. It took a second glance for me to see that there was a picture designed in the tiling.

"The Taylor Crest," I whispered to Philip, who stood looking pleased beside the blinking butler.

He nodded. "Yes. My grandpa—multiplied by four—had that done. It was a present for his youngest son, who was going to die of tuberculosis. Tommy loved the crest and wanted it added to the art of the house. More than just the flag on top of the roof. So...." He waved at the floor.

"I bet every inch of this place is laced with Taylor history."

"Every centimeter," Philip corrected. "I'll tell you all about it after we meet with my parents."

"Right."

14

DEVASTATING BLOW

We walked down the long hall branching off to the right, heading for the library. Each employee we passed stopped to stare at us. Philip would nod as we passed and say something to each one. I would smile but said not a word.

Philip stopped before an oak wood door forty feet down the hall. He looked at me and swallowed hard. "This is it. Now that the time's come, I'm scared."

I squeezed his shoulder—I'd already gotten a shock about my parents; we were heading into a situation that might give him one. "I understand completely. If you want, I'll do all the talking."

He shook his head. "We're in this together." He reached out a slightly shaking hand and opened the door. Both of us stepped in at the same time.

I looked around. The room was huge and smelled of book leather and cedarwood. It was carpeted with thick, lush, hunter-green carpet, and ceiling fans were stationed periodically around the room. But there were no people.

Philip tipped his head to the left. "My parents have a favorite spot. They'll be there."

Before heading out to find his parents, I closed the door behind us. I saw a lock and flipped it—this was something I didn't want an employee to barge in on. Turning around, I walked side by side with Philip around the magnificent fountain, dominating the center of the room, over to a large window seat where Mr. and Mrs. Taylor sat enjoying a book.

My first real look at the Taylors was everything I had expected it to be. I saw two wealthy but modestly dressed adults. Mrs. Alicia Taylor wore a long, navy blue dress with a modest neckline. She wore prudent heels (prudent meaning she could walk in them without fear of breaking her ankle) and a single strand of pearls accompanied by a matching pearl broach, bracelet, and earrings. She was laughing at a picture her husband had pointed to. Mr. Justin Taylor was smiling at his attractive wife and looked handsome himself in navy dress pants, a designer red polo, and shiny black leather shoes.

Philip and I stopped four feet away, and he cleared his throat to get their attention. "Mom, Dad, I'd like you to meet a friend of mine."

Neither one looked at us at first. Mr. Taylor, closing the book, apologized, "Oh, Philip, we're sorry we didn't see you come in— we were looking at our honeymoon pictures."

He turned back from putting the book on the shelf behind him. Mrs. Taylor looked up at us too. Both were speechless and pale as they stared at us standing before them. Our left hands were in our pockets, and we were standing in the same comfortable position. We looked more alike than we ever had before.

"Dad, Mom, this is Jesse Target. He's the friend I've been hanging out with for the past couple of weeks. We met at Twin

Pines on Donor's Day when I was almost beaten up. The boy thought I was Jesse."

Mrs. Taylor's face was gaining some of its natural color again. "My word, you two look so much alike!" she exclaimed. "It's incredible!"

Philip looked from one parent to the other. "It's not too incredible. Not when you consider Jesse's a blood relative."

Now the Taylors looked puzzled. "What do you mean, Philip? He's a cousin we never knew about?"

Philip faltered and looked at me. I could tell he wasn't sure how to ask his parents about how they came to be missing a child. I understood his uncertainty; the DNA test confirmed we were biological children of the couple in front of us, yet they seemed oblivious to the fact I was their son. Why were they trying to pretend like they didn't know I was theirs?

I took up the tail for Philip. "Mr. and Mrs. Taylor, I think you should sit back down. What we're about to tell you might not come as a complete shock, but it will shake you up." With confused looks, they followed my advice. Philip pulled up a couple of chairs and sat down. I found I was more at ease while standing, so I neglected the offered chair.

"All my life, I was happy to think of myself as a born-and-blood Target." I pulled my medallion out from under my shirt and handed it to them. They fingered it speechlessly. "I had no idea what this was until Philip told me. You can imagine how shocked we both were."

Mr. Taylor looked up, a look of complete bewilderment on his face. "What does this mean?"

Philip couldn't take the strain any longer. "Dad, Mom, we know about each other—obviously. He's standing right here!" He waved the envelope containing the test results in front of him. "We had DNA tests run to confirm it and everything! Why are you acting like you don't know who he is? We just want to know why."

Mrs. Taylor lost what color she had gained. She moaned and waved a hand in front of her face. For a second, I thought she was going to faint, but she squared her shoulders and shook herself. "Philip, you're not making sense, son. What DNA tests, and why is he wearing your medallion?"

Mr. Taylor held out his hand. "May we see that paper, please?"

Philip handed it to him. He waited, nervously perched on the edge of his chair. I stood loosely and watched the emotions cross their faces as they read the sheet. First, there was the look of confusion they'd been wearing. Then a look of perplexity. Then a look of awe. Finally, they looked up at us, their expressions settling on a mixture of all three.

"I don't understand," Mrs. Taylor whispered, looking from one of us to the other. "There were *two* of you?"

Mr. Taylor shook his head. "Philip, from the proof written on this paper, I can understand why you're demanding we explain this to you. You must be thinking we had twins, and then for some reason, gave one up for adoption." Philip shrugged helplessly—what else was he supposed to think? "I don't know why either of you should believe what I'm about to say with proof like this in front of you, but you *have* to believe us when we say this paper shocks us even more than it does you. On my word of honor, I promise neither of us knew there were two babies inside your mother. As far as we ever knew, there was only Philip. We can't imagine what happened."

"What about ultrasounds?" Philip countered. I could sense he wanted to believe his parents' innocence, but he wasn't stupid. I also think he was trying to make it up to me when he said my parents must have kidnapped me. He didn't want his parents to be the bad guys, but he didn't want mine to be, either. "I know you had one. How can you explain that?"

Mr. Taylor glanced at his wife. It was Mrs. Taylor who spoke. "Philip, we can show you the ultrasound right now; two babies were never clearly distinguished. Honest to goodness, we didn't know about Jesse."

That is possible. I reasoned. *I've heard about cases where one twin is blocked by the other the whole pregnancy. Since we were identical, it makes even more sense. I don't think she's lying about that.*

The look of anger that suddenly fell on her face convinced me she wasn't. "If we had known, we'd have *never* given him up! Philip, you know we wanted more children but couldn't have any after your birth. Why would we ever give up a son if we wanted more than we could have?"

Philip shook his head, shrugging helplessly. "Then how do you explain it?" The Taylors had no answer, which was a good thing, in a way—at least that cleared my parents of any wrong-doing. I hadn't been kidnapped.

So what did happen? I wondered while I stepped away from the family to let them take a moment to get their emotions under control. My mind was busy as my eyes scanned the huge room. I rubbed my chin. *Who split us up in the first place? And how?*

Philip was asking his parents that very question.

Mrs. Taylor shook her head. "I don't know. I'm too upset to think clearly about the past." She looked at me; there were tears in her pretty blue eyes. "I had another child to hold, to love. And for some reason, someone stole him from me even before I knew he was alive."

Mr. Taylor nodded. "Why would someone do such a horrible thing?"

I turned to face them again. "Maybe we should ask the person who gave me to the Targets."

All three Taylors looked at me blankly.

I was starting to put pieces together, ferreting out clues, and matching them with facts. "I wasn't put up for adoption then adopted sometime later—the Targets thought I was their born son. As far back as I can remember, they were always telling me how proud they were to have a son. They, like you, Mr. and Mrs. Taylor, couldn't have any more children. They were so happy to have a boy to carry on the bloodline and the Target name. I wouldn't keep the bloodline going if I were adopted. They thought I was theirs."

"But when were you given to them? Wouldn't this lady know her own child from someone else's? All it took for me was holding Philip in my arms one time, and I knew him from a thousand others."

"Mom had a C-section," I said thoughtfully, as more pieces fell into place. "Just like you, Mrs. Taylor, and on the same day, probably around the same time, if my theory is right."

"What *is* your theory, young man?" Mr. Taylor asked.

I explained everything. When I finished, I waited for a reaction.

Philip asked, "Do you really believe that, Jesse? It sounds kind of wild."

"This whole thing is kind of wild, but it's the only thing that *could* have happened, isn't it? Your parents didn't know, and my parents didn't know. The probability of me accidentally ending up with the Targets is very slim. What other explanation is there?"

Suddenly, Mrs. Taylor stood and reached out an arm to receive me. I studied her for a second before walking forward. She laid a loving hand on my shoulder then circled me with her arm, holding me tightly. It felt weird to be held by a strange woman, but I reasoned that she *was* my blood mother, and she could probably use the hug right now.

"Can Jesse spend the night with us? Please, Mom and Dad? That will save us time tomorrow when we do the confrontation.

Jesse can wear some of my clothes and sleep in my room with me. Okay?"

They smiled at him, then at me. "Of course Jesse can. It only makes sense, doesn't it? He's part of our family now."

While I was pleased that they would accept me without question, my heart jerked at the thought. My blood belonged to the Taylors', but my heart belonged to the Targets. What did the future hold for me?

15

EXPLANATION

I woke early the next morning, as I had trained myself to do many years ago. I rolled over to face Philip, who laid on the other side of the king-size bed we'd shared. He was still sleeping deeply, but I wasn't surprised—why should he be wide awake at five in the morning? Especially after the emotional rollercoaster he'd been on last night. First thinking his parents were hiding something, then finding out that they weren't, then discovering someone had taken his twin brother at birth and given him to another family. Yes, sir, I'd say he was done in.

I rolled onto my back and locked my fingers behind my head. Staring up at the ceiling, I thought about what would happen later today. What would the culprit's excuse be? How would he justify stealing a baby and giving him to someone else? Was my theory correct, or was there another baby, now teenager, out there somewhere in the world who truthfully belonged to the Targets?

I sighed deeply. What a mess that would be.

I laughed softly. What was I thinking? That this man made a profession from handing off other people's babies? Right, I needed to let down on caffeine if I was thinking so crazily.

Three hours later, Philip rolled over. He blinked twice before fully coming awake. He sat up, rubbing his right eye and covering a yawn with his left hand. "Hi. What time is it?"

I looked up from the book I had borrowed from him. "Eight-fifteen."

"How long have you been up? You look ready to take on the world."

I grinned. "No, just one man." Sitting up straighter in the comfortable armchair, I shrugged. "I've been up for a while. Picked out your outfit—it's laid out to the letter in your mini-mall."

He squinted. "My what?"

I smiled. "Your closet."

"Oh! Huge, isn't it? I could live in there and be just fine." He sprang to his feet and softly padded over the thick carpet into his walk-in closet. He came out ten minutes later wearing white jeans, white T-shirt, white socks, and white high-tops. "Did you have a white convention?" He teased.

"Yup. You had two white jeans, T-shirts, high-tops, and socks. It looked perfect."

"Perfect for what?"

"When babies are born, they put them in white blankets, right?"

He shrugged. "I guess so."

"So, we're in white."

He shook his head, grinning.

"It's a good thing yesterday was a Friday," he stated, sitting beside me. "Otherwise, you would have had to go back to Twin Pines, and we would have had to wait until school was done before going."

"When do your parents—" I was having a problem remembering that they were now *my* parents, too "—normally wake up?"

"Around nine."

I nodded. "Not bad. I expected much later—you too, for that matter."

"You have a lot to learn."

Not as much as he thinks. I can live just like any one of his friends if I knew the basic facts. This realization struck me as funny for some reason. I could—I really could fit in any social circle if I wanted to. I'd been a street punk, city boy, country boy, rich snob, and almost everything else in my secret life.

"What are you thinking about, Jesse?" Philip asked. "I have the strangest feeling. What is it?"

I sobered quickly. So, Philip really was receiving Jesse Best signals. This was dangerous; I'd have to be extremely careful.

I grinned mischievously. "Find out."

"How am I supposed to find out? I can't really read your mind."

I leaned back smugly. "Too bad."

"You mean you're really going to torture me with this tingly feeling and never tell me what it is?"

"Let me see," I tapped my chin thoughtfully. "Yup, I think so."

A knock on the door interrupted Philip's retort. We both turned. Philip called, "Who is it?"

"It's your parents," came the muffled reply.

We looked at each other. "I thought you said nine?"

"I did—they're up early." He raised his voice. "Come in!"

The door opened and in walked the Taylors. "Wow," Mr. Taylor said, stopping short.

Mrs. Taylor laughed. "This is going to take getting used to, walking into a room and seeing two boys that look alike."

We smiled at them.

"So, are you ready to go?" Mr. Taylor, wearing gray pants and a dark blue, casual long-sleeved V-neck sweater, asked.

"We thought we'd go out to eat this morning if you boys were ready," Mrs. Taylor added. She wore a green skirt and white blouse, with dainty ruffles on the cuffs and many pleats down the front. "We don't want to waste a minute of time—we've lost fourteen years with two sons, we aren't going to lose another minute."

I bit my lip—it was as I'd feared last night. Everyone seemed to believe I'd lost something by not growing up a Taylor. Even Philip felt that way, though he tried to be sympathetic to my feelings. I didn't see it like that. While not millionaires, I'd always had a family, and they gave me something the Taylors never could—Jesse Best. Would they ever understand that *I* hadn't lost something, even if they had?

"I'm ready."

I looked up. "So am I."

"Then let's go."

We left Philip's room, walking down at least a million hallways before leaving the mansion and getting into the family limo. It was really cool. It was painted powder blue—the Taylor color—and the Taylor Crest was painted on the doors.

We ate a speedy breakfast at House of Waffles before getting back into the limo and being driven to High Meadows Hospital ten after nine. It wasn't busy at that time of day, so we had no trouble parking. "We'll be back when we finish our business, Tony," Mr. Taylor told the older driver as we left the car.

We went straight to the information desk when we got into the air-conditioned building, where a middle-aged woman read some papers.

"Excuse me," Mr. Taylor asked, "is Dr. Marlow still in the maternity ward?"

"Yes, sir, both Dr. Marlows came in five minutes ago."

"Is she busy? We need to talk to her."

"No, sir, go right ahead."

"Thank you."

As we walked down the hall, I turned to Philip. "Why did your dad say 'her'? Dr. Marlow's a guy."

"That's Sir Dr. Marlow—Madam Dr. Marlow did my mom's C-section."

I nodded, a thoughtful expression on my face.

"What?"

"Let me think about it. I'm starting to think things are becoming even clearer than they were last night."

When we came to the door, Mrs. Taylor knocked. "Come in," came a woman's voice. Mr. Taylor opened the door and walked in with Mrs. Taylor. According to the pre-laid plan, Philip and I stayed outside.

"Why, hello, Mr. and Mrs. Taylor. What can we do for you?"

"Well, we would like a little information."

"Certainly. Won't you sit down?"

The Dr. Marlow I knew added, "What's the problem?"

"First, we'd like to introduce you to someone." Mr. Taylor raised his voice. "Boys, why don't you come in?"

Philip and I walked into the room side by side. We stopped before the L-shaped desk, slipping our hands into our pockets. "Hello, Dr. Marlow," we said.

There was no surprise on either doctors' face. They took one look at us, and Sir Dr. Marlow said, "Ah, Jesse. You found the meaning behind the medallion. I knew you would one day." He sat down wearily. "I can't say it's not a relief. It's been a continual strain on my wife and I ever since the Targets passed away. We wanted to tell you but were afraid."

"Your wife was in on it, too?" The minute I knew there was a Madam Dr. Marlow, I'd thought she had to have been.

He nodded and glanced at his watch. "It's too late for breakfast and too early for lunch.... Why don't you all accompany my wife and I to the doctors' lounge, and we'll have coffee or soft drinks. We'll tell you all about it then."

In ten minutes, we all sat around a round table in a lush doctors' lounge, drinking soft drinks or coffee for the adults. We waited impatiently for the two conspirators to begin their story.

Madam Dr. Marlow was the first to speak. "The whole thing was my idea. I convinced Carl to go along with it." She looked at Mrs. Taylor. "I did your C-section at the same time Carl was doing Jenny's. Jenny Target was little more than a kid—twenty-five. She ran into complications. The baby—a little boy—died right after the C-section began. There was nothing to be done to save him.

"When I learned of the death, it tore my heart out. I knew how much a baby had meant to the Targets; they could never have another one and had no money to adopt a child." She dropped her head. "I know what we did was wrong, but I couldn't get the picture of Jenny Target's sparkling eyes out of my head. I felt compassion for her. She hadn't done anything to deserve what happened to her, and yet her only chance of motherhood was gone. That's when I thought the whole scheme up."

Sir Dr. Marlow added, "We both agreed on it, so it's really both our fault. Miriam first suggested it, then I helped it happen. You see, we thought since you didn't know you were going to have twins, we could take one of your sons and give him to the Targets. No one would ever know since you were asleep when the babies were born, and Jenny was asleep when her baby died— she'd naturally think it was her very own son. You'd be none the wiser. So instead of having a mother with two babies and one empty-handed, there'd be two mothers with a baby each, and everyone would be happy."

In my seat across from him and beside Philip, I leaned back with the tiniest nod. I had guessed right. Everything I'd theorized yesterday was being confirmed today. But I had a question that wasn't being answered.

"Dr. Marlow, why did you give me the Taylor Crest and tell my parents to tell me it would insure me a future? That part doesn't make sense. We may have found out while my parents were still alive, and you'd have been in trouble."

Carl covered Miriam's hand with his, caressing it gently. "After the substitution, we began to feel guilty about what we'd done. We'd taken a wealthy child and placed him in a middle-class family. We worried about what would happen to you if anything ever happened to the Targets. When we heard the Taylors were giving Philip a medallion of the Taylor Crest, we knew that was the answer. We had an identical one made for you. We felt better after giving it to you. All you had to do was figure it out, and you'd have a sure future. We knew when you did work it out, our whole plot would unravel, but we couldn't stand by thinking that something bad might happen if we didn't risk it and give you the medallion."

"So, all this happened because you wanted to give a young mother and father happiness?" Mr. Taylor summed up.

"Yes."

"Are you going to press charges against us?" Madam Dr. Marlow asked. "We know that must be a form of kidnapping."

Were we going to press charges? Good question. I knew what I would do if I were the adults, but what would the Taylors do? Would they understand my view of things? It's not like you're given a "what-to-do-when-you-find-out-you-had-twins-and-one-was-given-to-another-family-to-make-everybody-happy" course in your last year of college. This was a decision they'd have to make out of the blue.

I had a feeling it was going to be tight. According to the facts, the Taylors were good people, but the way Mrs. Taylor had looked at me when she found out I was her son made me wonder if they would have the Marlows tossed in jail.

Mr. and Mrs. Taylor looked at each other. The room was quiet for several minutes as husband and wife had a silent conversation. Philip was looking at his hands. The Marlows were silent, and I was sure a little tense, while I sat on the edge of my seat.

Mrs. Taylor looked away from her husband and back at the waiting couple. "Last night, I was angry and hurt to learn Jesse had been taken from us. I wanted to come here and demand answers and rave at you—but that was before I knew why you did it. I think I can accept what you did as a charity mission and know that it was done to help someone, not to hurt us."

"I agree with my wife; this actually did no harm. We were happy with Philip, and the Targets were happy with Jesse. Now, Jesse's with us, and the Targets must have been good to him. He's a good boy." He smiled at me, and I ducked my head, blushing.

"So, you're not going to have us thrown in jail? You're not going to tell the head administrator and have our licenses revoked?"

"No. I think we'll quietly let this go since you were only thinking of making someone happy. But next time something like this happens, don't act rashly. Maybe we'll all be able to set something up that will help everyone the right way. Who knows, but someone might leave an 'abandoned' baby on the doorstep or something."

The Marlows, very much relieved, laughed merrily. "Who knows?" they agreed.

"Well, we have a lot of catching up to do with our new son, and I'm sure you two must have work to do. We'll get out of here and tend to some other matters."

We left High Meadows Hospital that day, leaving two very happy, relieved people. I imagined it might be the first time in fourteen years they could have a clear conscience.

"What now, Dad? Mom?"

Mr. Taylor smiled. "We catch up with each other. We have a lot we want to discuss, and I'm sure Jesse has a lot he must be curious about, right, Jesse?"

I grinned and nodded. "Right, sir."

"Can we go to DDT to catch up?" Philip asked as we got into the limo.

I stared at him. "DDT?" I couldn't believe it—Philip wanted to go to an outlawed poison plant to catch up?

The Taylors laughed at my expression.

"Daisy's Delicious Treats," Philip explained. "It's the best ice cream parlor, plus other treats, in the world. Everybody calls it DDT to make things seem dangerous. It's much more fun telling your parents you're heading for DDT than Daisy's Delicious Treats."

I let out a breath. "Whew, for a second, I was starting to worry about you."

DDT turned out to be a cozy place in the mall. It was tucked between Teresa's Tiaras—a jewelry store—and a bookstore called Merdis. It held up to its reputation of having the best ice cream in the world. Their chocolate chip mint left my mouth watering for more.

As we sat in a corner, both enjoying our ice cream, I asked something I'd been wondering about for several years. "What do the words at the top of the medallion mean? I've tried to look them up, but I've never found similar words or letters."

Philip laughed. "Of course not—it's not a known language."

I cocked an eyebrow.

"It's another piece of Taylor history. The first-ever Taylors had a daughter, the youngest of thirteen kids. Whether it was a mental disability, or if she just liked to stand out and get lots of attention, she acted strange. She'd wear her brother's pants, go horseback riding in the middle of the night, wander off, stuff like that. One thing she continually did was make up words and talk to herself in a strange language.

"Well, Silly—her real name was Sybille, but she wanted to be called Silly—died when she was only fifteen. No one wanted to lose her presence or forget her memory, so as a continual memorial to her, they put these words around the top of the family crest. They mean '*All for the Glory of God our Savoir*.'"

"Neat."

"It's been the Taylor motto ever since."

Mr. Taylor got to his feet. "Well, since we're all done here, why don't we head back to *Blessed Rest* until lunchtime?" He smiled at me. "I thought we'd celebrate Jesse's reunion with us by eating out at our favorite restaurant: *Bliss'*."

Mrs. Taylor nodded. "That will be wonderful."

"I need to call Twin Pines," I announced as we left DDT. "Mr. Hoffman will think I ran off. He's particular about knowing where everyone is all the time."

"I understand that," Mr. Taylor said with a nod. "We're kind of the same way ourselves."

I smiled. "Good. I won't have to worry about Philip."

When I finished talking, Mr. Taylor asked to talk to Mr. Hoffman for a few minutes. I gave him the phone and stepped aside. As Philip and I stood with Mrs. Taylor waiting, I heard him say I'd be spending another night at their home and wouldn't be back in time for morning chapel. He wasn't supposed to worry because I was behaving just fine.

16
STRANGER AT BLISS'

Philip and I spent the rest of the morning touring Blessed Rest on golf carts. I'd only seen part of the magnificent estate when lunchtime came, and we got back in the limo to head for Bliss'. The whole way there, Philip talked about the awesome food they served. He highly recommended their steak and chicken combo and their seafood dish. Just as we pulled up to the stylish restaurant, we decided we'd order one of each and then share.

The second I walked in the door, I knew the Taylors were known by first name here. They were shown to a table on a low dais without even having to say a word. When we were seated, friendly greetings were exchanged. I found out the young waitress was named Melody.

She glanced toward Philip and me as we sat together. "Oh!" she gasped. I smiled innocently at her astonishment.

Philip smiled too. "Melody, I guess you haven't met Jesse yet." He glanced at his dad, who nodded. "He's my identical twin brother. Didn't know I had one, right?"

She shook her head, and the bright smile was back. "No, I didn't. Where have you been hiding him all these years?" She extended her hand and said sunnily, "Hi, I'm Melody Walcott."

"Pleasure, Miss," I said cordially, inclining my head and shaking her hand.

She laughed. "I like him." She cocked her head and raised a skeptical eyebrow. "Is he really your twin, Philip?"

Philip nodded. "Yeah."

"We'll tell you all about it, Melody," Mrs. Taylor assured the bubbly brunet. Melody nodded and left to seat another customer.

"Is this place famous?" I asked after we were served monstrous plates of steaming food.

Philip swallowed a sip of red cream soda before answering. "Not too famous, but lots of upper-class people come here to eat. Why?"

"Well, since we sat down, three other families came in, and it's only been fifteen minutes max."

He shrugged. "It's a great place. The food is excellent, the staff very friendly and courteous, they serve *incredible* homemade ice cream, and it's a non-smoking/alcohol environment. It's a real family place."

I nodded. "I noticed the TV's only play clean stuff. I like it here."

"Good, because we eat here a lot," Mr. Taylor told me.

While we ate, we discussed me again. Mr. and Mrs. Taylor were endlessly curious about who my parents were, what my life had been like before meeting Philip, and just about everything else about me. I told them all about Jesse Target's life—it sounded just like every other normal boy's.

When we were finished, Philip offered to pay the bill while the rest of us went to the car. As the Taylors and I walked toward the door, I felt eyes on me. They weren't warm, and they weren't cold. They were the type I trained myself to be vigilant around.

I tried to pinpoint the section they came from so that I could pretend to trip and catch my balance while looking at the person at the same time. Just when I had the watcher pinned down to the left side near the back by the oil paintings, Melody came after us with an expensive fountain pen. She handed it to Mrs. Taylor, who thanked her, saying she must have dropped it.

I took the diversion to turn around as if I wanted another look at the place. I swung my eyes around the room inconspicuously. I almost missed him. He was a lone man sitting at a corner table reading today's paper. He looked like he had nothing better to do on a Saturday afternoon other than read the sports section. His mistake was glancing up right when my gaze swept over him.

He didn't look down quickly like guys in the movies would have done. This was real life—they were much better trained. He nodded his head politely before casually going back to his paper.

If I hadn't been so highly trained, I wouldn't have thought anything of the trivial encounter. But I *was* highly trained, and I trusted my gut. I didn't know him from any outstanding warrants, and I wasn't on a case to have earned someone's suspicions. Even so, I wasn't going to just forget him. I'd recreate his face and run it through facial recognition software once I got back to Twin Pines. Perhaps I'd get a hit.

"Jesse," Mrs. Taylor touched my arm lightly. "Are you ready?"

I turned and smiled at her. "Sure, just taking another look at the place. It really is terrific."

She smiled, giving my shoulder a small squeeze. The three of us walked out and got into the limo, and Philip came a minute later. Mr. Taylor gave directions to head back to the estate, and we were on our way again.

After dinner that night, we went into the living room. It was during this time that my world was torn from its axle and sent hurtling into outer space.

Philip, chipper and bouncing now that everything had worked out so nicely, declared, "You know, Mom and Dad, I always felt my room was too big, but now that Jesse will live in it with me, it's just the right size!"

My heart sped up. *Not good. Not good at all.* I had known this would have had to happen, but what a nightmare it would be! I was never supposed to be adopted, and here, I bumped into my twin and *wham!* I was being put into a *famous* millionaire's home. *Definitely not good.*

Mr. Taylor nodded determinedly. "On Monday, we'll take care of all the necessary details to arrange Jesse's reunion with the family." He squeezed his wife's hand affectionately. "He's going to be a lawful Taylor, and we'll never be separated again."

Philip beamed. "You'll enroll at High Crest with me, Jesse, and we can be in all the same classes. I can't wait to introduce you to all my friends!"

I beamed back at him, but secretly, I had my doubts—many of them.

17

JESSE TARGET/BEST: MILLIONAIRE

"We'll come in before your room is given away to get all your gear, Jesse," Daisy promised on Tuesday morning, the day I was to move into the Taylor estate officially. It was the first chance we'd had to freely talk since I left two days ago; Philip had been sticking to me like glue. He was so eager to have me move in that he hadn't left me alone since we started packing. I'd finally convinced him to bring one of my bags down to the waiting limo to give Daisy, Ace, and me enough time to wrap up a few details concerning Jesse Best.

I sighed, looking around the familiar room. "Thanks." It was the first time I didn't have to pretend to be excited about moving away, and I know my voice sounded pretty deflated.

Daisy put an arm around my shoulders. "This isn't the end of your secret career," she encouraged. "We'll work something out, and things will get back in balance. Be patient and see."

I smiled at her. "Thanks, I'll try. Oh, before Philip gets back, there's something I need you guys to run on my criminal-finder." I pulled out a detailed sketch from my waistband and handed it to Ace. "That's the face of a man who was watching me while at *Bliss'* on Saturday. I don't know him right off, but I want you to check him out, see what you can find. He was one of those luke-warm watchers—the kind that never means nothing."

Ace nodded, taking me seriously—he knew the gut reaction as surely as I did. He'd do what I wasn't going to be able to. "We'll send you the results via coded message."

"Thanks, I appreci–"

"Curtain!" Daisy warned sharply. "Philip's coming!"

Ace stuffed the picture into his shirt as Daisy moved from watching the door. I pretended to be lifting a box of models. When Philip walked in, the curtain had come down on Jesse Best and up on Jesse Target.

"Thanks again for helping me get packed and ready to go," I said to Ace and Daisy. "And thanks for all the things you did for me as my Floor Parents."

Ace smiled and squeezed my shoulder, telling me to have a good time in my new life. Daisy wiped a tear from her eye. "We're both so very glad you found your family, Jesse, but we'll miss you terribly. You were always my favorite." She hugged me around the box I held. "Come back and visit us at times, won't you?"

"I will. Goodbye." Philip picked up the last of my things, and we turned and walked out the door.

"They sure like you."

"Yeah, they were like my grandparents. I'll miss them."

Philip looked at me closely. "Jesse, you *are* happy you'll live with us, aren't you?"

"Of course—why did you even ask?"

"Because at times I feel like you wish you could stay here, then at other times, I get excited just from the excitement I feel from you."

I knew I sounded convincing as I said, "I *am* excited. It will be great living with you and your parents, but I'll miss Mr. Ace and Miss Daisy. That could be why you feel I don't want to live with you—it's when I'm thinking about them."

Philip started to say something, but I spotted a group of teens heading up the stairs. They'd run right into us if we continued our route. "Detour," I hissed and turned Philip around to hurry to the service elevator at the other end of the hall.

"If we'd let those kids see us, they'd never have let us leave," I explained, pushing the button on the panel marked with a *G*. "This way, we'll be out of here long before they know we've left."

"Oh," he looked around. "But isn't it prohibited for kids to use this elevator? It was marked Staff."

"I got special permission to use it today so we could avoid the kids—Mr. Hoffman didn't want you getting mobbed."

Philip sighed deeply. "I hope you're ready, Jesse."

I turned to him. "For what?"

He looked me in the eye and said seriously, "To be rich. Welcome to the life of the millionaire."

The life of the millionaire, I mused, as yet *another* kid came up to me and shook my hand, welcoming me to my new school and telling me how we would be great friends. Just before slipping away, the boy hinted about his "need" for a dirt bike. *What a life it is.*

"I warned you," Philip whispered as we could finally leave the huge building and walk along the school campus. "Everybody wants to be with you because they want to get their picture in the school paper, and you're the hottest thing around."

"I think I got my picture taken at least twenty dozen times," I agreed good-naturedly.

It was my second week at Philip's upper-class school at High Crest Academy. The first week, everybody had been shocked by the double vision suddenly placed upon them. Now the surprise had worn off, and I was famous. Philip barely had time to introduce me to his *real* friends before I was grabbed and towed down the hall to meet another bunch of kids who wanted to be my "friends."

A camera flashed from the bushes to our right.

Philip and I turned to face each other. "Twenty dozen and one times," we said, then laughed and continued. At the end of the sidewalk, two of Philip's genuine friends met us.

"Hi, guys," too-thin Steve Pitts greeted over his stack of books, which slid to the right and were in danger of crashing to the ground any minute. The tall boy with brown eyes shoved a shock of sandy blond hair from his forehead. "Was today any better?"

Henry Bates, best described as a fat-bottom/skinny-topped peanut with horn-rimmed glasses and freckles, shook his head. "With those buzzard reporters? Things could only get worse." He looked at us. "Am I right?"

Though very pessimistic, Henry promised to be a fun character; his dry humor was great for a hard day. I had liked him and Steve from the start. To reply to Henry's gloomy inquiry, I nodded. "I counted at least twenty dozen-and-one pictures, and half the student body came hitting me up for something or other."

Henry looked triumphantly at Steve. "See? I told you." Steve rolled his eyes.

Honestly, I'd been cast into a very interesting lot. None of Philip's friends was anything alike. Steve was optimistic and bouncy, while Henry was pessimistic and heavy. Philip was everything I was except a detective/agent. And the last of Philip's real friends was....

Allis Billson, the one I knew I would have trouble with. With every movement he made, he exuded dislike for me. I didn't know if it was the fact I had just recently become a millionaire and he thought me beneath him, or if he just didn't get along well with strangers.

"Hi, guys. Jesse."

Ah, nothing like a friendly greeting to make you feel warm and united with your twin brother's friends! That was Allis. He'd just come up from the sidewalk leading from the chemistry lab, and as always, he greeted his three friends with a heartfelt, "Hi guys," and me with a detached I-despise-you, "Jesse." I wondered if the others had noticed and just not said anything.

"Hi, Allis," Philip said. "What took you so long? You're five minutes late."

Allis shook his crow-black head remorsefully. "I nearly couldn't come at all. You know Ben James has been picking on me ever since I was given the key to the chemistry lab?" The guys nodded; I had no idea what he was talking about. "Well, he tried to trap me into getting detention for the entire week," he grinned broadly, "but his plan backfired. Now he's getting detention, and I'm free to go to DDT with you."

"Wow, what did he do?" Steve asked, as we began to walk toward the parking lot, where the limo drivers waited to take us to the ice cream parlor.

"He put a rat in Sherri Maxwell's desk with a note tied to its neck. Sherri fainted, and the rat got away. It took us half the period to catch the stupid pest, and when we did, the note was there for the entire world to see. It said, 'Ha, ha, sweet vengeance.' That nearly got the key taken from me. No one could have put the rat in the desk during normal hours, so it had to have happened before the lab opened, and only I have a key—besides Mr. Spencer, of course."

"So, they thought it was you?" Henry stated.

"Yeah. Luckily, I had alibis, and someone had seen Ben coming out before the lab opened today—otherwise, I'd have been dead," he groaned at the aspect. "My parents would have totally killed me."

When we got to DDT, we sat in a booth I soon recognized as a favorite. Personally, it drove me crazy. My back was turned to the window, exposing myself to any possible gunplay. I couldn't see if a sniper was out there, or anyone else for that matter, so I was a sitting dead boy if it ever really happened.

After we ordered, the boys got to talking about a camping trip up in Michigan. It seemed they did this every year during High Crest's special holiday, Liberty Weekend. They'd fly there in a private helicopter right after school ended on Wednesday, then come back late Saturday night. While they were gone, their parents would get together and do something. It sounded fun, but I wasn't sure how things would go since Philip, Steve and Henry were all enthusiastic about me coming this year, and Allis was his normal I-despise-you self. I'd just have to wait.

The week that would end in a three-day weekend camping trip in Michigan came. That week brought great enthusiasm and excitement. Even my coming along couldn't keep Allis from jumping a little on Monday as school let out.

That night, the three boys came over just to make sure we had everything. They all spoke at once in excitement. It kind of felt good to see them like this; it helped me remember that just because they were rich, that didn't mean they still didn't act like normal fourteen-year-olds.

But then came something that would tear my newly reestablished world apart once again. We were all sitting in Philip's and my personal living room in our suite of rooms, enjoying an old comedy, when my cellphone rang.

"Sorry," I apologized and got up to go into our bedroom. Closing the door, I glanced at the return number—I didn't recognize it. Flipping it open, I thought it would probably turn out to be a wrong number. "Hello, Jesse Target speaking."

"Jesse Best." I froze, holding my breath. "North Avenue, 927, Elko, Nevada." The man hung up.

Closing the phone woodenly, I slumped against the wall. I was being called for a case, and I had no idea what I was going to say or how I was going to get away.

I straightened up determinedly. I was the "best" —I'd find a way. It didn't matter if I were the son of a millionaire, someone was in trouble, and the lawman blood in me would not rest until I'd helped the person with whatever I was needed for.

18
ON MY WAY

A moment later, my cell rang again. I flipped it open, knowing what I'd hear and who would be telling me my directions. "Jesse Target," I said into the phone. I knew it would be Daisy or Ace, but there was a slim chance it wasn't, and I'd been taught to call myself Jesse Target even after getting a call until I knew for sure whom I was talking with.

Daisy's clear voice came over the phone. "Detective Jesse Best, you mean."

I sighed in relief. It would be so much easier being a detective than being an agent and sent first to Nevada, then to another country. "What's the status?" I asked, pulling my shoe off and opening the secret panel that carried my mini-recorder. I hooked it to the phone and waited for Daisy to begin.

"I know we've been through this a million times, Jesse," Daisy began, surprising me. What about my orders? Why was she saying this? "But this is the first time you've been called up since becoming Jesse Target-Taylor-Best. We figured you would need a little help from old-timers on this one."

"What do you mean, Daisy?" I glanced at the door to be sure none of the others had followed me out.

"Last time we talked, you told us you still hadn't found a way to get out to go on cases, so we've figured it out for you." I stood there listening without interrupting, even though I wanted to ask questions. "You told us Philip's going camping this week-end, and his parents are leaving town to visit some friends in Washington." Her voice got mockingly apologetic. "You'll have to miss the campout this year, Jesse. You see, you're going to fall sick the night before, but tell Philip not to worry or cancel the trip. You'll be fine because you'll go stay with your Twin Pines' Floor Parents since the employees are off for the weekend. Tell him to have fun and not to worry about you; that you'll be fine and will go next year."

A slow grin had begun to spread across my face while she spoke, and now it was a fully-fledged smile. Leave it to my counterparts to help get me out of a bind. "Thanks, Daisy, you really saved me a lot of trouble."

"That's what we're here for, remember? Now, when you go to school tomorrow, you'll walk by a professor on your way to science class. He'll be tall, stern-looking, balding, and wearing wire-rimmed glasses and a gray suit. He'll pass you a small item that looks like a package of sticky-tack, then he'll disappear.

"Here are the directions to the drug—when you get home from school, go to the bathroom, rip the package open, and eat one of the six squares. You'll feel lousy for twenty-four hours, but after that, you'll be on your way to Nevada."

"I've got it," I affirmed when she paused. "Now, what's this case about? What's my objective?"

"You're going to visit your long-lost uncle. Unfortunately, you find out he just recently died. Baldwin Brown, your cousin and new owner of the estate, invites you to spend the weekend with them, even though your uncle is dead. Under that guise, you'll do the snooping. This is what's going on: valuables are disappearing from the family estate. Baldwin doesn't know how or who's stealing them; there are a few suspects and theories. You're being hired to find out what's going on. We'll give you all the files you'll need to read when you get here tomorrow afternoon."

"Okay."

"You'll have to work fast, Jesse. You only have two days, three at the most."

"I know."

"But don't worry. After all—you are the best."

I grinned. "I'll see you in—" the handle on the door connecting me to the room with the other boys turned, and the door began to open. "*Curtain*," I hissed and hung up the phone, hastily removing my recorder and shoving my shoe back on—I'd replace the recorder in its rightful place later. As for now, it'd be safe in my pocket.

Philip stuck his head out the door, a mixed expression on his face. "Is everything okay?"

"Yeah, sure, why wouldn't it be?" I asked innocently, slipping my cell back into my pocket to cover the mini-recorder.

He shrugged. "I don't know. You were gone so long, and I got this funny feeling. I wanted to make sure everything was all right."

I put on my most convincing grin. "Sure, I'm okay. I do know what feeling you meant, though. Are you sure it didn't come from you and transmit to me?" I joked.

I had never known school to be so boring or so long in all my life. Now that I had a plan to get myself out of here, I wanted to get moving. Two days wasn't very long on anyone's calendar—even for the best, it would be hard to figure everything out in that short amount of time. I needed every second, and it seemed that with each passing minute sitting at a desk, they were slipping away.

I was sure my watch had broken when it said it was the normal five minutes to two when we finally headed to science class. I kept my eyes open for the professor as I walked beside Philip. He spoke about the camping trip, so he didn't notice when a tall man wearing a gray suit came toward us.

As he was supposed to, my contact looked stern, but there was a barely noticeable undertone of worry. He looked from Philip to me, to Philip again. I guessed he didn't know which of us he was supposed to pass a drug to. I couldn't blame him; even Daisy and Ace hadn't been able to tell us apart, and they'd lived with me for two years.

When he looked at me again, I caught his eye and nodded the tiniest bit. He tipped his head to affirm he knew it was me and reached into his pocket casually. When we were two feet away, he withdrew his hand and lowered it to his side; I mirrored the movement. As we passed, our hands brushed, and a plastic-wrapped, two-inch square was slipped into my hand. I nonchalantly placed my hand into my pocket again, and the pass was done. No one was the wiser.

Following my instructions, I went straight to the bathroom when we got home. Closing the door tightly, I pulled out the package. The content was bright yellow and divided up into little squares. Opening the flap at the top, I slid the square up and tore off the cube I was supposed to, popping it in my mouth.

I knew it was a good thing that drugs don't taste good, but as I tried to swallow the bitter-tasting paste, I wondered why drugs like this tasted vile. I mean, detectives are *supposed* to eat them—couldn't they get a good flavor?

Finally, I got it down and went to hang out with the others, who sat around the mini-living room, talking excitedly about the camping trip.

I joined in the conversation and waited for the drug to take effect. Just thirty minutes later, my head started to throb, and my stomach felt funny. I tried to keep talking but fell silent; all my thoughts were on how lousy I really felt. If I hadn't known I'd taken a drug, I'd really think I was sick. This stuff was wonderful—in a sick way.

"Hey, Jesse, are you all right?" Philip asked when he noticed I'd dropped out of the conversation and was rubbing my forehead.

I looked up at him. "My head hurts, and so does my stomach."

Face full of concern, he got off the beanbag and came over to me while the others looked on. He put his hand to my forehead. "Wow! You're hot; how long have you felt bad? I haven't felt anything all day."

At least drug-related sicknesses didn't transmit, or we'd have been in trouble. I shrugged as Philip told Steve to get a thermometer. "I guess it came on suddenly. I was fine all day, but thirty minutes ago, I started feeling like this."

"Put this under your tongue," Philip directed when Steve returned with the thermometer. Obediently, I did. A moment later, Philip pulled it from my mouth and looked at the degree. He whistled. "101.5. You need two aspirin and bed."

I didn't argue. Henry brought the aspirin with a glass of water. I swallowed it, then allowed them to guide me to my new single bed. When I was in the middle with the blanket pulled up to my chin, Henry's gloomy voice lamented, "I guess we can say goodbye to our campout this year. We'll have to stay here to nurse Jesse."

"What? He's fourteen! He can handle a school bug without needing all of us to 'nurse' him," Allis complained.

"Someone's got to stick around, Allis," Steve countered. "All the employees have the weekend off, remember?"

"Oh, yeah." He sent me a withering glare.

Like it's my fault I got sick, I thought hotly.

Philip cut into the banter about staying or not staying and hiring someone to watch me with, "You guys can still go; I'll just stay here with Jesse."

"No way! It wouldn't be the same if we didn't *all* go."

"He's right," I moaned. "You can't let this ruin your vacation. You all go, I'll be fine. It probably *is* just a twenty-four-hour thing I picked up at school."

"Then what will you do after you get better?" Steve challenged. "We'll all be off hobnobbing in the wild while you're here by yourself and lonesome. We can't do that."

"No, that's not how it will happen. We'll see if I'm not better by the time you guys leave. If I am, I'll go along as planned. If not, then I'll go back to Twin Pines and spend the time with my Floor Parents. They'll love to have me back, even if I am sick. This way, everyone gets their planned vacation."

"I can't leave you like that!" Philip protested.

"Why not? I don't mind living with my Floor Parents for a few days."

"Because I'm your twin brother, and as such, I have to stand by you when you're sick. What else are twins for?"

I smiled weakly at him. "Thanks, Philip, but I don't want to ruin the trip just because I got sick. Go. Have fun. I'll be all right until y'all get back, and I'll come next year—we'll have a great time the next camping trip."

"I think that makes perfect sense." Allis agreed.

It took a lot of talking, but finally, Philip gave in.

The next day, Philip and the boys went to school—Philip still fretting about how he wanted to stay with me—and I went to Twin Pines to get better on Daisy's marvelous chicken soup.

The drug was starting to wear off by the time I walked into Daisy and Ace's room. Daisy had her chicken soup ready, and Ace had a file. He gave it to me while I lay on the couch, sipping the steaming broth. "This is everything we've managed to scrape together. It's not much, I'm afraid, so you'll have your work cut out for you."

I nodded and opened the file. I read the sheets of paper once, then reread them, making notes in the notebook I always carried. By the time I finished, I had a good idea as to where to start.

From what I'd read and what I could read into it, three different motives could be behind the thefts. When "Uncle Francis" died, he had given his entire estate to his youngest son, Baldwin. Francis cut three older kids out of the will for his own reasons. The eldest was Macklin, who'd always been bossy and wasn't popular with the employees. He had been heir until Baldwin was born and won Francis' heart—his motive would be revenge.

Then there was Maggie. A glamour girl, she thought at least a portion of the estate should be hers because of the way she'd manipulated people to do business with her father. Her motive would be hatred.

Lastly, there was Todd. He had been his mom's favorite and promised half of the estate when his father died. He'd always had a violent temper, so when Baldwin got the entire estate and he'd been left with virtually nothing, he'd threatened him, telling him he wouldn't have "his half" very long. His motive was jealousy.

Just as I finished reading and making notes, my cellphone rang. I nodded for Daisy to pick it up. She waited a discreet three rings, then said, "Good afternoon, this is Daisy Jackson speaking. I'm talking on behalf of Jesse Target.... Oh, it's you, Philip, dear! ... No, I'm afraid Jesse's still under the weather. He's resting on the couch right now. Do you want me to ... oh, all right, dear—have fun camping. Jesse will be fine when you get back.

Bye-bye." She hung up. "Philip just wanted to make sure you still didn't feel well. He says they are leaving, and he still wishes you were coming or he was staying."

I smiled. "I love my twin brother."

"When did you take the drug? Right after you got home like you were instructed?"

"Yes."

"You should be basically well now." She looked at her watch. "Your flight leaves in two hours. Let's get going."

19

DINNER OF SUSPECTS

An hour after a smooth flight to Nevada, I stepped out of the plane with several other passengers. I looked around for my "cousin," who would be picking me up. Before boarding, I'd been given a description of Baldwin Brown. He was in his early twenties, with brown hair and brown eyes. He'd be wearing a navy blue suit.

I spied him before he spied me. Actually, he looked right past me, as if still searching for the person he was here to pick up. I grinned inwardly—I got that a lot from my employers. Everybody expected someone grown-up.

Shouldering my duffle bag, I walked uncertainly toward him, pretending to be unsure as to who he was. I cleared my throat as I approached. Squinting up at him, I asked in a hesitant voice, "A-are you my uncle, Francis Brown?"

Baldwin looked at me, startled, a look turning to one of almost shock. "Is *your* name Jesse Best?"

I grinned at him. "I thought you'd be a lot older, Uncle Francis."

I gave him points for levelheadedness. He gathered himself in one moment, then laid a mockingly sympathetic hand on my shoulder. His face told anyone looking that he was about to tell me some bad news. He was a good actor. "No, I'm not Francis; I'm his son, Baldwin. I'm so sorry to have to tell you this, especially after your long trip, but my father—your uncle—passed away."

I stared at him, pretending to be stunned beyond words. After a moment, I feigned a recovery and shook my head. "Are you sure? Why would he invite me all this way if he were going to die?"

"I think he thought he had more time. I wish you would have been able to meet him, but just because he's no longer alive doesn't mean you have to leave right now. On the contrary, I want you to stay at my estate for at least a day or two. Then you can go back to your mom. This way, the entire trip won't be a waste."

"Sure, sir, that's … that's fine."

He shook his head in feigned sympathy at my dazed expression. "Come, I'll take you to my limo." He took my arm, leading me through the crowd and to the parking garage. Once the doors were securely closed, Baldwin turned to me and said skeptically, "You're a famous detective? You can only be twelve years old."

"Fourteen. All the same, I *am* a detective."

"But you're a kid. How could you be everything I've been led to believe?"

I leaned against the plush seat. "A kid, as you call me, can do things unobserved an adult could never do. Watch. As I work, you'll see no one pays me much attention. If I were an adult, things would be different."

"All right, but what do you plan to do to keep my estate from being plundered?"

"First, tell me when this plundering started."

"Three weeks ago. I noticed one of my father's favorite portraits missing in the library. I thought maybe one of the maids had taken it down to dust, but when it wasn't returned, and I found other valuable things missing as well, I knew someone was taking them."

"What did you do about it?"

"Naturally, I questioned the employees—none of them knew anything about it. They said they thought *I* had taken the things and moved them somewhere else."

"You have three older siblings. Did you question them?"

He shook his head. "No, they don't even know things are missing. They live in their own homes and seldom visit mine now that Father's dead." He looked at me. "I suspect one of them is the thief. All three were fiery mad when I was given the majority of Father's estate. They all thought they were more entitled to it than me. You see, my dad devoiced their mom to marry mine. They think of me as the son of a dead gold-digger who robbed them of what they should have had. In their opinion, I should have gotten the least of all of us, if anything at all."

I nodded thoughtfully. "Do you suspect any of them above the others?"

"I can't say. Macklin is the eldest; he should have inherited everything, but when Father found out about his gambling, he wrote up a new will. I think Macklin blames me for it—I was the one who told Father about his obsession with horse racing. Then there's Maggie—she never liked me because I disapproved of her business methods. Lastly, there's Todd. His mother spoiled him, and he always had this special hatred of me." He sighed. "All three have plenty of reason for doing it, I just don't know which one it is."

"That's what I'm here for."

He looked at me. "Yeah, I just hope you can get to the bottom of this before all the valuable things are stolen right out from under me."

Ignoring his continual doubt of my capabilities, I asked, "How do you think the thief is taking the things? Your estate must have security."

"Both guards and systems. That's why I think it must be one of my half-siblings—they know the codes, and when the guards change; they'd be able to sneak in and out without detection."

I nodded, thinking about what he'd told me and what I'd read. "Squeezing things a bit, I have three days to figure this out. First, do your half-siblings know I'm coming?"

"Yes. I pretended to find a correspondence in Father's belongings between you and him. I pretended you've been writing him for several months. I even wrote up phony letters, just in case someone demanded to see them. Your mother finally told you who your uncle was after running away with his younger brother and being unofficially disowned. You decided to write him because you wanted to know more about the family."

"In that case, the first thing I want to do is read all the letters, so I know what I'm supposed to be like." He nodded. "I suppose I'll be grown-up."

He flushed a bit. "The letters you wrote do make you sound a little older than you turned out to be." He shrugged. "You can always say you wanted to sound older because you didn't think he'd have anything to do with a child."

"That's a possibility," I agreed, admiring his quick mind. "After I'm brought up to date, I want you to have the others over to introduce me. I want to know who each one is and see if I can pick out anything from their actions and behaviors."

"I'll invite them over for dinner."

"Excellent."

Three hours later, I laid down the last letter. I looked at Baldwin, who had been sitting on the chair watching me. "I commend you on your letter writing. If I didn't know you wrote these, I'd be convinced Jesse Best from Halifax did."

"Thank you."

"I am a bit curious. Why did you choose Halifax for the place my mother and father ran away to?"

He shrugged sheepishly. "I guess I just let my imagination run wild. I must admit it was fun creating you. I've never done this before."

I smiled. "Ever consider being a writer? From what I've learned about you in the past three hours, you'd make a great one."

He blinked. "You know, I never thought of that." The doorbell rang and continued to sound. "Oh, that will be Macklin—he always leans on the doorbell."

"Very considerate," I mocked as I put all the letters into the satchel at my feet. "Be cool, sir. I'm just your long-lost cousin."

He nodded, wiping his hands on a handkerchief. "Why don't you call me Baldwin?" He winked. "After all, we are cousins."

"Where's the little twerp?" a voice growled behind the door separating us from the entryway.

"Which twerp are you referring to, sir? Master Baldwin or the visiting Master Jesse?"

"Will you ever learn, Toby? Baldwin isn't a *master*—he's an upstart tramp. I'm not talking about him this time; I'm talking about this new tramp Baldwin's dug up. Probably wants his *share* of the estate like all the others."

"Oh, no, sir! This young child is a gentleman. He's got good raring."

"I'll judge that for myself. Just show me where the scamp is, okay, Toby?"

"Yes, sir."

The door opened, but before Toby could announce Macklin's arrival, the stocky man barged in. I guessed him to be twenty years older than Baldwin, but his scowling face made him look much older. "So, you've dug up another skeleton, have you, Baldwin? You can never leave anything alone; you and your meddling will have the estate depleted in no time. The honor the rest of us have tried to live up to will be squandered away with you living here."

Baldwin must have been accustomed to this kind of ridicule because he didn't flare. He politely smiled as if greeting a pleasant dinner guest. "Good evening, Macklin. I hope you're well—"

Macklin turned his back on him and stalked over to me. The letters had depicted a bold young man, so I got into my role by offering my hand to the glowering stranger. Instead of taking my hand, he grabbed my chin and looked me over, turning my face from left to right. "Well, he doesn't look like a tramp. Doesn't look much like my uncle, either." He dropped my face, turning his back on me. He marched over to the big easy chair Baldwin had been sitting in before getting up to greet his less-than-pleasant half-brother. "Time will tell what this boy is made of, if he deserves to hold the family name."

The doorbell rang again. This time, it was three short blasts.

"That would be Maggie."

A moment later, I heard a dull voice droning, "Yes, I know I'm late, darling, but it's only a dinner party at Father's ex-estate. Nothing important, after all." The door was thrown open, and a woman wearing a flashy black dress came in. She was talking to Toby over her shoulder. "So, Toby, what does this child look like? If he looks anything like my uncle, poor thing. I remember Uncle Laurence—oh!—what an ugly man. I was shocked any woman *ever* fell for him—" Her words cut off when she turned and saw me. A smile curled her thin, red lips. "Oh, my! How precious." She swept toward me, throwing her arm over my shoulder and petting my cheek. "So adorable! I could just take you home and keep you forever!"

"He's not a cat, Maggie."

She continued as if Baldwin hadn't spoken. "Oh, what a charming little thing you are. Ten years old, maybe? I simply must keep you for the charity banquet next week." Her eyes flashed with devious glee. "Think of all the heartstrings I can pull with him by my side!" She looked at me. "You don't mind if I call you an orphan, do you, darling?"

"Ma'am, I'm fourteen," I corrected with disgust. I pushed her hands away from me. "And, no, you can't call me an orphan." The lying cheat—no wonder Baldwin hadn't approved of her business dealings.

She didn't catch my dislike of her and tried putting her arm around my shoulders again. What did she think I was? A stray dog that needed cuddling? "Oh, but no one needs to know that, darling. Come now, it would only be one evening. What do you say? Be a good boy, and help out your poor cousin?"

I removed her arm from my shoulders and stepped away from her. "My mom is very much alive, and she'd have my head if she found out I helped cheat people."

Baldwin's miffed voice cut in. "He's not a pet, so stop treating him like one, Magritte." The brunette turned glowering eyes on her half-brother. Before she could lash out at him, the doorbell rang a third time.

Doorbell saves the day once again! I thought, as Maggie moved from my side to sit in a huff on the couch.

No dialogue was heard before the doors banged open, and a wiry young man marched in. He could only be a few years older than Baldwin. He said nothing to anyone—just looked around the room. His eyes stopped on me. He looked at me coldly, then marched over and grabbed my hand. "Todd Brown, kid. Hear you're Unk's kid, come all the way from Halifax. Must be disappointing to come all this way to meet your father's brother only to find you have to put up with a grabbing poser. What's your name?"

Talk about rudeness. Not one of the Brown children had an ounce of manners or respect for anyone but themselves. I wondered how Baldwin had escaped this side of the Brown inheritance. "I'm Jesse Best, sir."

"How come you're not a Brown? Unk take a new name?"

I nodded. "My mother's name—they adopted it as their own when Father was disinherited."

"And now you've come to take revenge, is that it?"

I blinked. "Why no, sir! I came because Uncle Francis invited me. I wasn't expecting to arrive to find him dead. I was looking forward to meeting him."

"I'm sure you were."

"I was! My father died when I was little, so I never really got to know him. I wanted to know his brother in the hopes I'd see something of my father in him." Behind them all, Baldwin smiled. This information had been written to Francis in my penultimate letter.

"Why don't we eat dinner?" Baldwin suggested, stepping in to rescue me from their accusing stares.

I watched every move the three Browns made all through dinner. As noted before, none had any manners, and all treated the employees as if they were dirt. I was glad the Taylors didn't act this way, or I might have had to disown myself. Poor Baldwin to have these three dragging his name through the mud.

The minute the three siblings left, Baldwin turned to me, rubbing his temples. "I'm sorry, Jesse—I didn't expect them to act like this."

I cocked an amused eyebrow. "Oh? You mean they were worse than normal?"

"No, they're always like that when around me, but the way they fell on you did surprise me." He scowled. "Especially Maggie! Why, if she weren't already cut out of the will, I'd disown her!"

I couldn't disagree to that.

He sighed. "So, did that help you any?"

"Not really," I admitted. "It did tell me something about their personalities, though, and you never can tell when that actually *does* help."

"What do you have planned?"

"First, I'm going to rearrange your security cameras. I'm going to tap into them and stream their images to the TV in my room—I'll be able to keep an eye on things that way."

Baldwin blinked. "You can do that?"

I grinned. "Of course."

Thirty minutes later, I was connected and well set up against the prowler; there wasn't a room in the entire mansion or a yard or garden I couldn't look at.

Baldwin was impressed; he kept murmuring how he couldn't believe his eyes. He ran all over the house with me, watching every move I made then asking questions about it. I didn't really mind—he wasn't getting in the way, and if he could listen while I ran around, he was welcome to come.

That night, I stayed up late flipping through channels, keeping an eye on things. I fully expected an attempt after tonight's dinner. If it were one of the siblings, they were sure to be worked up. They'd be raring to soothe their anger by stealing something, I was sure.

Around midnight, the door to my room opened. I flipped the TV to a sports channel before turning to see who it was.

"Hard at work, I see," Baldwin teased, grinning. He was standing with a tray of late-night snacks and mugs of hot chocolate.

I grinned back at him. "Come in, if those cookies are for me."

His eyes sparkled with fun. "They were, but now that I see how well you're taking care of things, I'm not so sure." Nevertheless, he walked in, closing the door with his foot.

Soon as the door was closed, I flipped back to surveillance channels. "I switched just in case it was a maid or someone," I explained as he set the tray on the nightstand then hopped onto the bed to sit beside me.

"Anything happening?" he asked, reaching for a cookie.

"Nothing yet. I'm sure something will, though, if I'm patient enough to keep watching." Noting the two cups and his getting comfortable, I raised an eyebrow. "You're sticking around to watch with me?"

He looked at me. "If you don't mind. This fascinates me. You're really good—much better than I'd ever thought to give you credit for before watching you work."

"Sure, you can stay. It's just surprising having a millionaire hanging out with a kid detective." I swallowed a gulp of hot chocolate. "You're not alone in finding out I'm worth the money you're paying me. All my clients are inclined to react that way at first."

We were both silent for several minutes as we watched the TV screen. I watched Baldwin out of the corner of my eye. I could tell something was bothering him. He looked as if he wanted to say something, but just as he worked up the courage, he chickened out.

Finally, I turned to face him, a small grin tugging up the corners of my mouth. "Baldwin, you can say it."

He blinked. "What do you mean?"

"You're perched over there, thinking about saying something, then biting back the words. Just spit it out."

He smiled. "You *are* perceptive." Then he sighed. "I was just thinking if this is what it's like to have a younger brother." He looked over at me. "You know what I mean? Hanging out all day, coming to watch a "movie" together late at night; most of all, being around someone who doesn't call me a twerp or a thief. It's been really fun for me."

I felt touched by his words. In addition, I felt like I knew what he was feeling, what he was saying without saying. I reached over, laying a hand on his shoulder. "It's been fun for me, too—it's not every day my employer hangs out with me." I smiled widely. "And I think of all the Brown kids, you're absolutely the best."

He grinned. "Thanks, Jesse."

20
NIGHT WATCH

It was approaching two o'clock when I got my first glimpse of the thief. Baldwin had fallen asleep soon after one-thirty and was still leaning against the bedpost, snoring softly. I had been leaning against the pillows contemplating how I could speed this up when the burglar's shadow fell across the rose arch in the east garden.

I sat up straight, pressing a button on the remote to bring the image closer. I peered at the screen a moment longer before taking my notebook and writing a couple of notes, all the while keeping an eye on the screen.

The outline was bulky, but I couldn't tell from this angle if the bulk was part of the body or something being carried. I reached for the remote with my left hand, writing an observation with my right. Swiftly, I punched in the channel that would show me the image from the camera posted on the wall facing the prowler.

Just then, the person walking silently toward the house passed under a garden light, illuminating his face beautifully. I grinned triumphantly—that would make a superb shot when I printed it off the tape. It was a perfectly clear image of Macklin Brown.

I was about to touch Baldwin's shoulder when more movement caught my eye. Interesting. It appeared to be Sam, one of the guards. He was walking straight to Macklin, and Macklin was waiting for him.

That solves how he's getting in and out without detection, I mused, jotting down Sam's involvement.

I watched as Macklin handed Sam two hundred dollars in twenty-dollar bills. In return, Sam handed him a key to the door he was supposed to guard. All this was conveniently done beneath the shining lamp. Once this was done, Sam disappeared into the darkness, and Macklin continued on to the back door.

I glanced at Baldwin, smiling at what he was missing but not daring to wake him because I feared he'd charge in and jump Macklin before he actually stole anything—that would ruin everything. We had nothing unless we could see him stealing something.

So I postponed waking him, watching in silence as Macklin entered the house. The camera lost sight of him here, so I switched to the next channel displaying the back entrance.

Macklin crept into the art gallery—one of Baldwin's renovations. I clocked his movements flipping from channel to channel. He went right away to the painting Baldwin spoke of during dinner. It was one of a kind he'd bought only last week, worth at least $50,000.

Macklin reached up quickly and removed the painting from its place of honor among others in its class. Just as he lowered his arms, someone flipped the lights on. Macklin turned his head, the smug snarl he'd worn while removing the painting still in place.

I couldn't see who turned on the lights from this angle, so I flipped to the previous channel. All I could see was a man's broad back. He wore the blue uniform of Baldwin's guards, but I knew this one wasn't Sam. My heart pounded. Had someone else solved the case before me? What would Baldwin think?

But as I watched, the broad-backed man entered the room, leaving the video's screen. Hastily, I flipped back to the channel depicting Macklin still holding the valuable painting. I couldn't afford to miss a second of this meeting.

Macklin stuffed his beefy hand into his pocket. I held my breath, ready to press the button to alert the staff of an intruder if he pulled out a gun, but it wasn't a weapon he removed—it was another wad of twenty-dollar bills.

I frowned. This man was working with Macklin, too? What was his job?

The man turned. The video caught a perfect view of his face just as he pushed the money into his pocket. My frown deepened. *Who is that guy?* I knew I'd seen him in the book of pictures of the guards that Baldwin had shown me earlier, but who was he, exactly?

As the light turned off, Macklin pulled a canvas sack from his shirt. I smiled; there went some of the bulk I'd seen earlier. He wrapped the painting inside the sack then headed back the way he'd come. I continued to follow him until he disappeared behind the rose arch he'd entered by. I wrote down more details quickly—times, how long it took to make the steal, how many people were helping, and so on.

As I wrote, I tried to bring the man's face to the front of my mind. I knew he wasn't very important; he didn't guard a gate or entryway. I'd gazed at his picture and name only for a moment before flipping the page.

Suddenly, I knew who he was. *He's the guy in charge of the surveillance room. Why is he getting paid?* I thought about it, going one way, then another. Then, out of nowhere, the reason jumped out at me. *Baldwin told me he was puzzled because there was never anything on the tapes to show break-ins. Each time he discovered some-thing missing, he watched the tapes for clues. He never found any.* Now I knew why. Macklin was paying Tom to erase the tapes.

My mouth dropped open in awed amazement. This guy had things worked to the tiniest detail. He got in, stole something, then paid another guard to rewind and re-record the tapes of the rooms he'd gone through. What a smart guy. If it hadn't been for my backup copies, we would have lost all the evidence.

I wrote that down. When I finished, I reached over and shook my employer's shoulder. "Baldwin, wake up."

After a second, the young man blinked his eyes and sat up groggily. "What's up?" he yawned.

I smiled triumphantly. "I know who your burglar is."

Now he was wide awake. "What? Who? What did I miss?"

I put on a look of sympathy. "I'm sorry to inform you that your new painting *Olas de la Mar* was stolen." He gasped. "And two of your guards are in cahoots with Macklin, who is the thief."

It took a moment before he recovered from the devastating news. When he did, he looked me in the eye. "Tell me everything."

I filled him in on all the happenings of the past half-hour. When I finished, Baldwin was stunned. "I never thought Macklin had the brains to come up with this kind of operation. Are you sure he bribed two of my guards?"

I nodded. "Yes, Tom Knox has probably already rewound and covered the recordings."

He groaned. "That means all the evidence is gone."

"No, it's not. He may have destroyed your security tapes, but he didn't touch the copies I made." I hopped off the bed and knelt beside it. Lifting the floor-length ruffle, I showed Baldwin, who knelt beside me, my bank of recording devices. "This is where I disappeared to while you were on the phone long distance. I have a copy of Macklin's theft and his bribery of Sam and Tom. We have great evidence."

He beamed at me. "Jesse, you're a genius! I think I'm going to have to raise your pay."

I laughed. "Not necessary; this is my job."

"So, what are we going to do? Show Macklin and the police the proof?"

"Not quite. It'd be way too suspicious if you had this kind of stuff the day after I came. It'd be better to wait a day before showing this to anyone." A different thought struck me. "Better still, let's not just show the proof—let's set up a trap for tomorrow night and have some police on-hand to arrest him. We could pretend it was all your idea; I'll be in bed sleeping when you and the police bust Macklin."

Baldwin cocked his head. "I like the idea of playing the hero, but how are we going to make this trap work? Macklin doesn't visit here twice in one week."

A slow grin curved my lips as an idea began to take form. "I think I know something that will have all your half-siblings here by noon tomorrow."

21
SETTING THE TRAP

"Macklin? Hi, this is Baldwin—" he paused as the oldest Brown interrupted angrily. I could hear Macklin shouting from where I sat, listening to Baldwin's first move to trap the sneaky rat. It was so loud that Baldwin had to move the phone from his ear. "Before you slam the phone down, you might want to hear why I'm calling you," he snapped, with just the right touch of annoyance.

I put a hand to the headphones I wore to hear the conversation—now that Macklin wasn't screaming his wrath, I needed to use the phones to hear. "Fine, Baldwin, but this better be good," he growled.

Baldwin turned and winked at me; it was obvious he was enjoying his part in my scheme. I grinned back at him, giving him a thumbs-up. His face took on an expression of utter seriousness as he turned to talk once more. "Something very serious has come up. It involves all us Browns–"

"Get it straight, Baldwin," Macklin snarled, "you are not a Brown! You're a slob who doesn't deserve—"

"I suppose Jesse's not a Brown either, then?" Baldwin shot back.

"What are you saying?"

"Just this. Today, I found a secret drawer in Dad's desk. You know the one: big, antique, he kept it in his office?"

"Get on with it."

Baldwin drew in a deep breath. "I found certain things in this secret drawer. Things like letters, notes, even a few pictures." He paused, just as we'd rehearsed. Then, "And a couple of certificates."

"Is this blubbering attempt supposed to tell me something?" I could hear a change in his voice; it grew colder with each word. Things were going as planned.

"Listen, Macklin; I'm trying to tell you in a gentle way that I discovered Terra Best secretly married Francis Brown shortly after my mom died. A few years later, Jesse was born—*from our father*. Jesse isn't a Best—he's a Brown. I have the documents to prove it. He's Dad's *son*."

There was dead silence on the other end of the line. I could almost see Macklin turning first white, then red. I glanced at my watch. *Three, two, one ....*

"*He's what?!*"

I grinned; Macklin exploded right on time.

"He's Dad's son—our half-brother, Macklin. From what I got from the notes, Dad met Terra Best at a business meeting. He was lonely, and she was sympathetic. One thing led to another, and they ended up marrying. After how your mother treated mine, it was decided to keep things a secret until we were all older. Jesse started writing Dad because Terra and Dad thought it was time to tell him the truth about who he is. The only thing is, Dad died before he could finish this."

Macklin made several sputtering attempts to speak but couldn't find his tongue. Now to put the bait in the trap.

"I want to give Jesse some of the inheritance. It's only fair, and I have a note that says Dad was going to update his will to include him. I'm going to fulfill Dad's wish and give Jesse *Break Away Haven* and the ocean cruiser that goes with it."

"You're giving away our family winter house in the Hamptons? Oh, no. No. Never in a million lifetimes—not without consulting all the family. I'll be there in an hour—we'll talk about this then." He slammed the phone down, terminating the conversation.

Baldwin glanced at the phone before setting it back in its cradle. He turned to me. "Well, I guess it worked."

"I told you it would." I took off the headphones. "Your half-siblings will explode at the idea; another half-brother equals even less inheritance for them. Macklin will go on a spree to get as much of your inheritance as he can. He might even try to get mine."

"Well, now," he rubbed his hands together. "We've called all my halves, and they all promised to be here in an hour. They should all arrive close to the same time. Where do you want to be when they get here?"

"I've got two options—in my room shocked, or screaming at my mom over the phone in here. Which do you want?"

He scratched his chin. "No doubt Macklin and the rest will want to attack you as they did me as a kid. You want to be chewed out while you're on the phone or supposedly shocked in your room?"

I grinned. "I know what I want, but what do *you* want?"

"You're the detective," he teased.

"You've been doing a great job so far, lining things up and giving life to my character. Which response do you think Jesse Best from Halifax would take?"

"You can be on the phone."

"Good—I want to be able to yell back at them. They might learn something."

"I doubt it."

I was watching from the window in the study when three limos, driving madly, screeched to a shuddering halt outside the front door. The doors flew open without waiting for the valet to assist them. Macklin, Maggie, and Todd leaped from their cars and flew up the steps, and barreled through the doors frantically. I looked at my watch. It was exactly one hour since making the first call.

I listened for the cue to pick up the phone and start yelling. Daisy was on the other side of the line, prepared with all the answers just in case any of the halves took the phone and wanted to talk to her for confirmation.

"Give him a break, will you?" Baldwin's sharp voice came through the door. "He's just learned his dad's not who he thought he was. He's in my office now, long-distance, talking to his mom."

I picked up the phone. "Curtain," I whispered to Daisy, who acknowledged. I could hear all three Browns talking at once, with Baldwin trying vainly to keep them out. Quickly, I began my act. "What do you mean, it was the best for everyone?" I yelled, making sure my voice rose higher and higher. "You secretly marry some millionaire then decide to hide it from me by moving to a different country?" I paused, listening while Daisy read off the answer sheet I'd emailed her. "Fine, it seemed the best option at the time. Whatever. But why didn't you ever tell me the truth? How could you lie to me for so long?" Again, I listened. "How can you say the right time never came up? I'm fourteen, Mom! There had to have been at least *one* time you could have told me."

Just then, the door banged open, and in tripped the Brown Trio. Baldwin came in last, still protesting and telling them to give me some space.

I gave them one of my best glares before turning back to the conversation. "Yeah? Well, I don't *feel* protected, Mom; all I feel right now is lied to."

Macklin snorted loudly. "All he feels is lied to, Maggie. Can you believe it? Only lied to."

"Oh, poor thing, you," Maggie cooed. It wasn't a pleasant sound. It was more like the baby talk villains in cartoons make when they tie the hero up and feed them to the sharks.

I sent them a withering glare but made no comment. "Mom, it's bad enough you lied to me, but you also tried to cover it up; that hurts almost as bad." My voice grew a little more iron-like. "You went and told me my *dad* is my uncle! Didn't you know I'd write him? Couldn't you see this would end up as it did? Come on, Mom."

"Oh, she knew it would end up this way," Todd sneered. "She's using you to get what she claims to be her right from *our* inheritance! Just like I said when you first came. I knew I smelled a rat."

"You couldn't tell a rat apart from your own ratty smell," I growled, covering the phone with my hand. "If I weren't on the phone, I'd deck you so hard you'd go through the floor." Todd's face turned scarlet. He stepped toward me, but Baldwin got in between. "Is that what you call it?" I snapped into the phone. "Well, I call it garbage."

"Just like you."

"Why don't you go get lost somewhere, Todd?"

"I got a better idea, twerp. Why don't *you* go get lost?"

Maggie crossed her arms. "Yeah, things would be better off for everyone if you just disappeared."

"Oh, I get it. Now that I'm your half-brother, you don't think I'm the adorable-take-home-forever-and-keep-as-your-pet type? Or do you just feel bad that you can't cheat people at charity banquets because I'm related to you, so obviously not a charity case?"

Her face darkened, and she clenched her fists. "Watch your mouth, kid. Just because your blood came from *our* father doesn't mean I can't slap your precious face."

"If it weren't for you, things would be so much easier for the rest of us," Macklin added coldly. "Why'd you have to go and get born? You're causing much more trouble than you'll *ever* be worth!"

I whirled around, crossing my arms over my chest. "Oh, so it's *my* fault your mom couldn't hold on to your dad and he fell for my mom?"

Before they could snarl a reply, Daisy's concerned voice came over the phone. "Jesse? Are you still there? Please, don't hang up on me."

Quickly, I turned my back on them and brought the phone back to my ear. "Sorry," I said curtly, then listened while she talked.

"Sorry is right. You're a mess if I ever did see one—just wait till the press gets a load of this!" Maggie faked a laugh. "They'll have a heyday! Just like last time. You two are doing a grand job of ruining the Brown name!"

"Shut up and leave me alone—No! Not you, Mom!" I glared at the seething trio. "I'm talking to my *new snobbish* half-siblings, who won't get off my back!" Their hatred deepened.

"Come on, guys, leave him alone," Baldwin ordered, herding them away while I continued yelling. "We have some business to talk about, remember?" That worked—they were off me and on Baldwin in a second. He led them out of the room and closed the door behind him.

Half an hour later, I dropped the phone back in its cradle. Jesse Best from Halifax was emotionally drained. Yelling at your mom, screaming at your half-siblings, learning the truth about your life—it all took a major toll on your energy. Right now, Jesse Best from Halifax needed a little peace and quiet. A long nap might help him, too.

So, I headed to the room I'd been lent; I'd deal with my half-siblings after recuperating. All the employees I passed gave me sympathetic looks—one even patted my shoulder. Inwardly, I was smiling; no one had a clue this was all a charade.

From the living room, I could hear the heated conversation— even from the second floor! I paused to listen for a minute. Baldwin insisted I be given my part of the inheritance, and the other three insisted I get nothing.

"They're fighting up a storm, aren't they?"

I turned warily to see that the elderly maid, who took care of my room, had come to stand next to me. "Don't you worry, Master Jesse—Master Baldwin will make sure you get your share."

I shook my head. "Right now, I don't care what I do or don't get."

She shook her head at me compassionately. "Poor baby. Is there anything I can get you?"

"No, but thanks. I'll be fine ... I guess." I turned and headed for my room. When I got there, I closed the door and lay down on the bed.

Three hours later, a gentle knock sounded on my door. "Who is it?" I called softly.

"It's Baldwin, Jesse. May I come in? Just for a few minutes."

"Sure, if you want." I sat up slowly.

He came in, locking the door behind him.

"Did it work?" I whispered hopefully.

He grinned and nodded. "Just like you said it would. They decided it was better we let you have valuable paintings and other things instead of the house in the Hamptons." He winked. It had all been part of my plan. He'd steer them to an option of giving me the house or letting me take my pick at the valuables. Of course, they'd choose valuables—people like them would want to keep a nice, cozy vacation house for themselves.

Now I would go through the house, picking out things Baldwin had directed me to earlier. Several of them were Macklin's favorites; he'd come to make sure I didn't make off with any of *his* things.

"You think your character feels up to going through the house picking out your inheritance? Or should we give you some more time?"

"When are your halves leaving?"

"Oh, I think they'll be sticking around for a while. Probably until you pick your inheritance."

"They just want to chew me out some more." I looked at him compassionately. "I'm really sorry for you, Baldwin. The Browns really take out the anger they have for their father on you. It's got to be tough. I don't see how you stand them."

He smiled softly. "Thanks, Jesse." He licked his lips. "Will it be okay with you if I keep up a pseudo correspondence with your character even when you leave? I want a brother who doesn't hate me."

"Sure you can; I'd kind of like that." Normally, I didn't get so close to my employers, but something about this man drew me. Maybe it was that he was enthralled with everything I did and went running around with me, setting things up and staying up late watching surveillance. Maybe it was his need for someone to love him now that his father was dead, just like mine.

I didn't know what the reason was, but an idea began to toy with my mind. I pushed it to the back of my brain to think about later that night. Now, I was on duty. "I think my character self can handle going with you now."

"Remember the things you're supposed to pick out?" He asked as I walked with him toward the door.

"Yep."

He looked down at me and laughed. "I'm sorry, Jesse, I know you're competent enough to remember a few trinkets. Guess I'm keyed-up."

"Don't worry about it." I patted his back. "I'm glad you're so into your role. Besides, even detectives forget at times."

22

THE WRAP-UP

After going through the house picking out things I'd like for my inheritance, I went back to my room to escape the constant nagging from Macklin, Maggie, and Todd. Baldwin, on the other hand, was a constant friend and defender. He was compassionate and kind; understanding exuded his every move and word. I had to hand it to him—he was good at acting. But then, he knew what the character me was going through. He was just doing for me what no one did for him when he was a kid.

I didn't go down for dinner that night; Baldwin had some delicious food sent up. I ate hungrily, as I hadn't gone down for lunch to keep up with my character's loss of appetite. While I gobbled down the roast beef, cooked carrots, potatoes, and onions, along with half a dozen rolls, I listened to the conversation going on in the dining room.

It was mostly banter. I did notice, however, that Macklin kept repeating how they were going to waste half the best things in the old house "on a little twerp." This made me sure he'd make his move. None of them knew when I'd be returning home again. They did know I had to get back in time for school, so that would goad Macklin into making his move tonight, just to be sure he got a chance in case I left tomorrow.

They left after dinner, and Baldwin came up to check on me. He stayed in my room, going over the details of tonight's hopeful bust. He wanted to make sure he had everything down.

We decided it was best I retire early after the wearying events of the day. Baldwin wished me good night, then left to tell the employees I was sleeping.

Instead of sleeping, though, I set things up for tonight's surveillance. As I worked, feeding information to the machines and changing wires, I thought over the plan. When he retired for the night, Baldwin would make the call requesting some policemen to come secretly to the house. They were to arrive after dark and slip in an open window on the mansion's east side. Baldwin would be there to meet them and tell them what was going on.

Well, not exactly—he would tell them what we *wanted* them to believe was going on. This was the story: he had noticed several valuable things missing over the past few weeks and decided to do something about it. He'd tell them he'd set up his own surveillance and show them the tapes I'd recorded last night. After that, he'd explain that he expected Macklin to make another strike. He wanted them on-hand to capture him and take him to jail.

An hour later, as I watched the screen monitoring the east side of the mansion, I saw seven men slipping from tree to tree. Zooming in, I saw they were the police officers requested to come. They walked over to the window and hopped in. A few minutes later, a red light flashed on my laptop. I quickly typed in the password, and then clicked to send the images over to Baldwin's TV we'd set up earlier.

While Baldwin showed the men the proof, I flipped through the surveillance channels. Baldwin's bedroom light had turned off by timer an hour ago; the house looked still and quiet. Macklin, Tom, and Sam wouldn't suspect anything—especially after I'd rigged the camera in the room Baldwin used to show a dark, empty room.

Ten minutes later, I switched the channel from the front of the house to the back. Just before the channel changed, I caught a glimpse of a bulky shadow separating from the hedge of roses. Quickly, I turned back.

Just like I'd predicted, Macklin, carrying several sacks to cart off his loot, crept toward the house. Just when I was about to give Baldwin a buzz, two more shadows separated, also carrying sacks. I stared at the screen incredulously. The two figures were none other than Maggie and Todd! Had they been stealing with Macklin all along? I quickly punched in a few letters then hit SEND.

Baldwin would be warned Macklin was here, and he wasn't alone. He'd flip to the station where he could survey everything I watched on my TV.

I followed the trio's movements across the driveway and around the fountain where Sam stepped out to claim his bribe. Macklin paid him quickly and started to move on, but Sam held him back. They talked. Sam kept pointing to Maggie and Todd; I guessed he wanted equal money from them.

It looked like I'd guessed right when Sam lifted the whistle he was supposed to blow if any intruders came onto the premises. Macklin grabbed the whistle, then jerked his head toward the grinning Sam. Todd and Maggie coughed up two hundred dollars apiece. Sam stepped back, then disappeared. The three siblings continued.

They walked up the stairs. They disappeared for a second while I changed views to capture them coming through the front door. Macklin came in first, looked around, then motioned the others in. They wasted no time about it. Macklin went right to the beautiful painting of Niagara Falls with twin rainbows and took it from the wall. Maggie went straight to a dainty alabaster box and slipped it gently into her sack. Todd picked up an Egyptian statue.

They moved to the study, where I'd chosen several paintings and figurines. I switched views again. They were about to move into the next room when Tom showed up, wanting his money. He must have been watching Sam over the security system, for he, too, expected two hundred from each. Once he got it, he left. Macklin led the way into the library, where a set of rare books was displayed and ready for me to take home.

I glanced down at my laptop to see what was happening at Baldwin's station. Two of the policemen were gone, probably dispatched to arrest Tom and Sam. The others were still watching the big screen TV.

I continued following the trio's progress as they went from room to room, filling their sacks with my inheritance. When all the sacks were full and all my inheritance, along with a few other things, were gone, Macklin led the way to the front door.

I looked to see what the police were doing—the room was empty. I searched for them until finding them, along with Baldwin, waiting to pounce on the unsuspecting thieves. They came loaded down with sacks, grinning about what they'd done.

Just as Maggie was about to open the door, the policemen descended. Whistles blew, orders were shouted, and with Baldwin, the police poured from every door. The three Browns stood frozen, shocked at the sudden arrest.

One of the police marched up to Macklin and relieved him of his burden. Two others did the same for Todd and Maggie. Then they slapped handcuffs on them, reading them their rights.

The missing policemen came into the room with Sam and Tom, handcuffed.

"I guess you won't have to worry anymore, Mr. Brown," the captain told Baldwin. "These guys are going to jail for a long time."

Tears streamed down Maggie's face, ruining her makeup as they fell. "Macklin, you promised us it'd be easy! You said it was a joke to get in and out! You claimed to have been looting the place for weeks!"

"Shut up, Maggie!" The oldest Brown snarled, sending dagger glares at her.

"Maybe you can tell our sister to shut up, but you can't tell me," Todd snapped. Turning to the policeman behind him, he said, "It's all Macklin's fault. He told us how he'd paid two men in Baldwin's estate to let him in and cover up his work. This is the first time Maggie and I helped. He recruited us because he said it was our *job* to make sure no twerp became rich with what should have been ours anyway."

Macklin exploded. "Oh, don't tell them I twisted your arm, dear brother. When you saw the brat pick your precious statue, you were all hands to grab it away from him and hide it in your mansion. And you, Maggie—you couldn't wait to get your hands on that alabaster box! Don't try to blame all this on me; I didn't force you to do anything!"

"Oh, yeah, and the fact that he wanted almost everything you did means nothing!"

Macklin was about to snap back at him when Baldwin broke in. "It's too bad all of you jumped the gun. Jesse and I made a deal about his inheritance. He said his mom and he didn't have the place for a bunch of antiques and stuff, so he'd let me keep everything if I paid him the worth. None of these things were going anywhere." That had been another part of the plan—it made it easy for Baldwin to keep his father's things and still make it look like I was getting an inheritance.

Macklin glared at him. "If it weren't for you, all this would have been mine. *Mine!* You don't deserve *any* of it!"

"Let's go," the police officer said firmly. He led the way, and the other men followed.

I grinned; it felt good to solve another case. Tomorrow night, I'd be flying home again, so I'd be at Daisy's when Philip and the others got back. I'd spend tomorrow with Baldwin, then get homesick and ask to go home to my mom.

Another case closed with a successful wrap-up, I thought as I slipped down into bed to catch up on some sleep. Tomorrow, Baldwin would tell me everything. I couldn't wait to get home and write this case down with all my others.

23
THE GREAT S.O.S.

'm sure going to miss having you around, Jesse, Baldwin's note said as we waited for the boarding call of flight 211. We were exchanging notes instead of talking so that no one could overhear us. Next, he wrote, *Especially now that I don't have any siblings at all.*

Looking up from my notebook, I smiled at him, writing, *You still have Jesse Best from Halifax. He's just with his mom now.*

He smiled, replying. *Yeah, but it won't be like I'll ever see him again. Unless another mystery comes up.*

I thought about the envelope in my back pocket. I'd give it to Baldwin before boarding the plane; it was something I didn't often do. In fact, he would be the fifth person I'd give this information to in all my years of crime-fighting. The first had been to an orphan Indian girl whom I'd rescued and gotten into a good Christian home after her uncle tried to sell her to the temple. The second had been to the Mexican boy I'd saved from his cruel kidnappers. The third to a spy on his way to execution; I'd nearly been blown to bits in that snatch/grab mission. The fourth to a set of twins who'd been pressed into gang activity and wanted out. Almost all had gone to kids with no parents or absentee parents. Baldwin would make the second adult.

The information in the envelope was an address and information to follow; I was giving him a ticket to contact me if he decided to write the real Jesse Best. Of course, he wouldn't write to "Jesse Best" or even to "Jesse Target;" he'd write to Tim Strickland: the lonely orphan boy I'd played to rescue Preetah. This boy lived at Twin Pines. Daisy would receive the mail, then send it to me now that I was no longer living there. Naturally, it wouldn't be a straight send to Twin Pines; the letters would go through several channels and safe networks before ever reaching the place I used to reside.

I wrote my next note with a straight face. *If a mystery should happen to come up, call your half-brother in Halifax—he has a knack for getting people out of troublesome situations.*

Baldwin grinned brightly. *You bet I will. I'm hoping something actually does come up. It would be fun to hang out again.*

"Flight 211 is ready for boarding. Flight 211 is ready for boarding."

I pushed my notebook into my pocket, picking up my duffle bag and extending my hand. "It's been real fun to visit you, Baldwin. Thanks for having me, even after Uncle, er, Dad died."

He shook my hand firmly. "It was a pleasure, Jesse. Come back any time you want."

"Thanks. Maybe I will." I turned to join the precession of people boarding. "Oh," I said, as if just remembering something important. "I still have your letter." I pulled the envelope from my back pocket and handed it to him.

He looked puzzled as he took it and scanned the name and address.

"You know, it's for that special friend. You gave it to me when you were unlocking the door. Good thing I remembered it."

He realized there was something special in the envelope I wanted to give him. Tucking it into his shirt pocket, he nodded. "Oh yes, thank you, Jesse. I would have been lost without this."

"Goodbye." I smiled and waved. He returned it. My last glimpse of Baldwin was of him waving goodbye.

I snuck into Twin Pines two hours later, heading straight for Daisy and Ace's apartment. I would have been earlier, except the flight hit major turbulence. We nearly had to set down!

I slipped through the door silently. I quickly checked around to make sure no one except one of my old Floor Parents was inside. It turned out not even they were there, so I laid down on the couch, closing my eyes to wait.

Thirty minutes later, or at least what I thought was thirty minutes—it's kind of hard to tell when you're cat napping half the time—the door opened. I cracked open one eyelid to see who it was. It was Daisy.

"I'm back," I announced, sitting up, startling her for a moment.

"Jesse!" She dropped her bag and rushed over to take a seat beside me. "How did it go?"

She'd learned long ago not to spout off a thousand questions when she wanted the details of the case; it only wasted her time and mine. She asked everything in one simple question, then waited for me to tell her the details.

When I finished, she got up to get me some orange juice from the fridge. While she poured juice for herself and me, I stated, "You'll be getting some mail from Baldwin, by the way."

She looked up, her surprise evident. "Oh? You must really like him."

I nodded. "I do. He hung out with me and helped. He wasn't like the typical employer. Besides, he's lonely. He's only ever had jerky siblings, and he liked Jesse Best from Halifax being his half-brother. He even asked if he could keep up a pseudo correspondence between my character and himself when I left. I gave him a real person to write to and receive mail from, so he won't be so lonely."

She smiled. "You're clever and thoughtful, Jesse." She held up a glass. "Juice?"

An hour later, the phone rang. Daisy picked it up and listened while someone spoke. Her face wore a frown that deepened the longer she listened. "Yes," she assured. "Jesse's here. He's feeling much better—*what*? When did this happen? ... Yes, Mrs. Taylor, no one but you. Okay ... okay ... see you in a few minutes." She set down the phone gently. I sat up and gazed deep into her eyes. I didn't like what I was seeing.

"Jesse, Philip's missing."

I sprang to my feet. "Tell me."

She shook her gray head slowly. "Mrs. Taylor didn't give details. She only said, 'Is Jesse with you? Philip's missing. We're coming over there to pick him up, don't let him go with anyone but my husband or me.' That's all."

I stared at her, refusing to believe her words. *Stop acting like a millionaire's son and start acting like a detective!* a sharp voice reprimanded. *Think of ways to find out about Philip. Stop wasting time like a dope.*

Nodding to the voice, I drew in several deep breaths. *Right. I have to step back and look at this through a stranger's eye.* I knew I'd never find anything if I kept thinking about my twin being lost somewhere.

"Paper? Pen?" I asked Daisy, who watched me closely. Smiling thankfully, she gladly handed me both. I sat down and began writing down ideas. True, I couldn't really do anything without knowing what I was dealing with, but I wrote things down for any possible dilemma.

First, I wrote for kidnapping. I remembered again the car that had followed Philip around. He'd said it was his parents, and nothing ever proved otherwise, so foolishly, I agreed. Now, with Philip "missing," I wasn't as sure. I also remembered the guy at *Bliss'*—he definitely held suspicion, at least for the time being.

Then I wrote for lost in the woods. I didn't know if foul play was the case or if he, even the other boys, simply got lost. Even if it were so simple, they would have to be found and rescued. I had no idea if they were equipped with survival methods or if they even knew *how* to survive on their own in the woods. I made a small notation to ask the next time I saw any of them.

Five minutes later, I heard feet pounding on the carpeted hallway floor. Seconds later, someone franticly banged on the door.

"That would be the Taylors," Daisy predicted. I hid the list of things I'd written under the couch and got up to meet Philip's parents.

They practically fell into the room when Daisy opened the door. They shot off a dozen words a second, Mrs. Taylor's face streaked with tears. Both Taylors looked pale. When they saw me standing by the half-wall that separated the entryway from the living room, they rushed forward, grabbing me in their arms.

"Oh, thank God you're still here!" Mrs. Taylor exclaimed, kissing me.

Mr. Taylor added, "We were so worried when the boys got back and told us Philip was gone."

"What happened?" I asked in a tight voice. Mrs. Taylor was nearly strangling me. "What do you mean, Philip's gone?"

My words set Mrs. Taylor off all over again. Daisy handed the distraught mother a tissue as I helped guide her and Mr. Taylor to the couch. Once sat, Mr. and Mrs. Taylor told me what they knew—which ended up being pathetically little.

"Everything was going fine the last time we heard from the boys," Mr. Taylor began, wrapping a comforting arm around his wife's shoulders. "They told us things were great. They were having a good time. Philip asked about you, Jesse." He shook his head. "That was yesterday morning. One of the terms of letting the boys go off on their own is they have to check-in each morning and evening. They missed their evening check-in, but we thought perhaps they were exhausted and hadn't thought of it."

Mrs. Taylor stopped crying long enough to chip in. "When they didn't check in this morning either, we got worried. We decided to send a helicopter to them early, just in case." Her eyes filled with tears. "Allis, Steve, and Henry were all at the campsite, but they told the pilot that Philip was gone." She turned away and sobbed into the tissue.

It was a good thing I'd dealt with other parents with missing kids; otherwise, I would have jumped up and strangled the answers from them. But being the best, I sat there, patiently waiting for them to go on.

"Allis and the others said they left Philip alone in his tent for thirty minutes while they cleaned the fish down by the creek. When they went to tell him it was time to cook, he wasn't there. Even worse, his tent was just as they'd last seen it—no sign of a struggle or forced exit. Philip just disappeared."

"That's it?" I demanded after they were silent for several minutes. "No footprints? No note? Nothing?"

"The boys looked around but couldn't find anything."

"They would have called sooner, but all forms of communication were gone, too. I'm so worried. Philip wouldn't have wandered off, and he wouldn't have taken all the cellphones. Something awful must have happened."

"I agree," Daisy nodded. "I haven't known Philip half as long as any of you, but I know he's not like this. This sounds suspicious."

"We've called the police but have nothing to go on. They told us they'd send someone over to talk with us, but when we remembered you were here, Jesse, we told them to send someone later."

"Of course, we explained we had another son and wanted to check on him," Mr. Taylor added. He squeezed my arm gently. "How glad we were to hear you were here and safe."

"But, where's Philip?" I wondered aloud. "Why was he taken?" I glanced at Mrs. Taylor.

"Perhaps he was kidnapped, and you'll receive a ransom note," Ace suggested, who had arrived in time to hear what was going on.

"I almost pray that is what happened. At least if we got a ransom note, we'd know Philip wasn't lost somewhere."

"Oh, and we'll pay the ransom, whatever they demand!" Mrs. Taylor cried. "Nothing is worth losing Philip." Her face, already pale, lost color completely. I was sure she would faint for one second, but then she stabled herself and grabbed her husband's hand. "Justin, I just had the worst thought! What if we haven't gotten a ransom note yet because they want Jesse, too? What if they're waiting?"

Mr. Taylor looked at me. A determined expression settled over his face. "If that is what they're doing, it won't happen. We'll find a safe place to send you, Jesse; you have nothing to worry about."

"Thanks," I said it as sincerely as possible.

Daisy and Ace shared a look. Ace turned to Mr. Taylor. "You know, sir, before my wife and I retired to be Floor Parents here at

Twin Pines, we were CIA agents." I gave them a guarded look. What were they planning? Never had they told anyone what they'd done when they were younger.

Mr. Taylor looked a bit surprised. "Oh, really? I never knew that."

Ace nodded. "Yes. If you wish, you can leave Jesse with us here. He'll be well-protected, and you won't have a thing to worry about. If anyone does come nosing around for him, we'll nab the person and send Jesse to a safe house I know of."

Mrs. Taylor's face brightened. "Would you do that for us?"

Daisy smiled her motherly smile. "Of course we would. Jesse means a lot to us, too."

My face looked as it had a minute ago, but inside, I was hopping—Ace and Daisy just gave me a passport to helping find my twin! Here, I'd be able to hit all the networks and run up all my contacts. This would be perfect!

"I feel much better already," declared Mrs. Taylor. She smiled for the first time. "Jesse will be safe, and we'll get Philip back soon. I know it."

24
PULLED

I went home with the Taylors to get a few things I'd need for my stay at Twin Pines. First, I packed a bag of clothes; then I retrieved all my gear that Daisy and Ace had snuck me two weeks ago. By the time I was ready to go back to Daisy's, the police had arrived and were questioning the Taylors and the three boys who'd gone camping with Philip. Henry, Steve, and Allis' parents were all with them, along with some men, who could only be bodyguards—these families were playing it safe with heavy-duty batteries.

I stood in the doorway, waiting to tell the Taylors I was ready to go. Just as I was wondering if I'd have to put up with a bodyguard, one of the policemen spied me. "Is this Philip's twin?" He asked Mr. Taylor.

"Yes, this is our other son, Jesse."

"Come in here a moment, son," the tall man requested. He motioned me forward then indicated a seat next to Mrs. Taylor.

I set my two bags down and walked into the room. I sat where I was told and waited.

"Did Philip ever express feelings of unhappiness or a desire to run away?"

I shook my head. "No, sir. Philip was always happy and telling me how great a family he has."

"Did he change after you came to live with him here and started receiving attention from your parents?"

"No, sir—he was overjoyed to have a brother." I glanced at his parents. "We used to stay up late talking about it and about how happy Mr. and Mrs. Taylor are with having another son."

The tall officer gave me a peculiar look. "'Mr. and Mrs. Taylor?' You don't call them Dad and Mom?"

My face flushed, and I dropped my gaze to stare at my feet. I'd never called the Taylors either name before—I just couldn't act like the two people *I* called mom and dad never existed.

"We've never really talked about that, Officer Black." Mrs. Taylor came to my rescue. There was something strange in the tone of her voice. I tried to pinpoint it but drew a blank.

"Oh." He cleared his throat. "Anyway—"

"Sir," I interrupted, "I know Philip didn't run away. I'm his identical twin, sir. He would have told me, or I would have felt something. I know it."

"We have to cover every base. There is no evidence Philip Taylor was kidnapped—"

"But he *was* kidnapped," I insisted, more confident now than ever. "I may even know who kidnapped him, or at least someone to check out."

All eyes were on me now. "What's this you're saying, son? What do you know?"

"Two months ago, after Philip and I had been meeting for a while, he told me a car followed him. He thought it was his parents because he hadn't told them about me. He thought they were trying to find out where it was he was going all the time. I believed him."

Officer Black stopped me to ask the Taylors, "Were you having your son followed?"

"No, sir. We trust our son."

He wrote on his notebook. "Continue."

"Well, the shadowing continued. Philip told me he'd seen three faces in his surroundings much more often than he should have. Again, we thought it was his parents. I saw the car once when he took me to meet them." I gave a quick description of the car I'd seen. "After I came to live here, the shadowing stopped. Or at least, Philip didn't mention it anymore. But I remember going to *Bliss'* my first Saturday here. I saw a man watching me—he was really good. When he saw me watching him, he just nodded and went back to reading his paper. Now that I think about it, he thought I was Philip since he was paying the check at the time."

"Why didn't you tell anyone before this?"

I slumped against the couch, not having to pretend one bit of misery at my own failure. "Maybe we should have told someone, but Philip was convinced it was only his parents. I believed him. Now he's gone."

"Jesse, would you be able to match the face of the man you saw at *Bliss'* with a man on our criminal records?" The officer accompanying Officer Black asked hopefully.

I nodded. "Yes, sir."

"You're sure?" Again, I nodded. "Then, if nobody minds, I'll take Jesse down to the station right away and show him some files."

Twenty minutes later, I sat before a computer next to Officer Parks. He went through all the possible suspects. None of the men matched.

"I sort of have this knack for drawing faces, Officer Parks. If you want, I'll draw you the man I saw."

"I think that would help a lot."

After drawing him a copy, he took me back to *Blessed Rest*, where I was taken to Twin Pines for an indefinite stay. No one bothered me as I walked up the stairs. It was dinnertime—everyone would be in the cafeteria.

I was the only kid in Twin Pines to have a key to Ace's apartment. I let myself in, then went right to work setting up my field base in Daisy and Ace's bedroom. I was an hour into my sleuthing before Ace and Daisy came in.

"Jesse? Is that you?"

"Yeah, I'm in your bedroom."

They walked in and looked around. "Not wasting any time, I see," Ace commented.

"Maybe too much time's already been wasted," I replied over my shoulder. "I'm pretty sure Philip was kidnapped." I went on to tell them everything about the shadowing. They agreed with my deduction.

"What came back on that guy I asked you to look up?"

"The one from *Bliss*?"

"Uh-huh."

"Nothing yet; we're still looking. So far, nothing's been found on him, but we'll double our efforts."

"Thanks. Let me know the minute you find anything."

"Will do."

As I'd told them my theory, they had been setting up their own equipment. Although they'd been retired for some time, they still helped the CIA occasionally, and they helped me. They got to work hitting their own highways.

"Oh, Jesse, I completely forgot!" Daisy exclaimed after an hour of silent work. "Did you eat dinner? Do I need to find you something?"

"Not hungry," I murmured.

"But you told me you didn't eat lunch…"

"S'all tite."

"What?"

"It's all right," I repeated, making sure to enunciate my words.

She sighed. "Okay, but if you get hungry, just tell me."

"Will do."

"And you will be eating breakfast," she firmly informed me, going back to her station.

I barely heard her.

The wee hours of the morning came, and we had yet to find anything. Nothing seemed to be happening anywhere. Worse, no one had seen signs of a boy looking like me with a man matching the guy at *Bliss'*.

I rubbed gritty eyes. Getting a total of six hours of sleep in three days while running full of adrenaline wasn't the greatest idea. I was completely wiped out but couldn't think of stopping until something came through.

"Jesse."

"Uh-huh?"

"Don't you think you need to go to bed? It's nearly four o'clock."

I tried to stifle a yawn that nearly broke my jaw. "I'll be fine."

"Jesse, you just misspelled your own name." She pointed to the mangled signature. "You really need some sleep before you mess up more words, if you haven't already."

"Daisy's right, Jess. You aren't going to do Philip or anyone any good if you're too exhausted to think clearly. Step back for a few hours and sleep—come back refreshed and ready. You are just coming off a case, you know."

"I'm not likely to forget that," I muttered. If it hadn't been for the case, I would have been with Philip and could have stopped this. Maybe. I wasn't actually regretting the case and meeting Baldwin; I was just thinking it could have come at a better time.

"No kidding, Jesse, you need some sleep. Daisy made the couch comfortable." He placed his hands on my shoulders heavily. "It's not just a suggestion."

I tipped my head back to look at him incredulously. "You're pulling me off the case?" I could hardly believe that! Sure, Philip was my brother and all, but that gave me more reason to find him. Why should he pull me?

"No," he assured. I slumped against the chair in relief. "I'm telling you to take a break. Now come on, or I just might pull you after all."

"Okay," I let him lift me from the chair and lead me to the couch Daisy had made into a bed, with my pillow ready and waiting for me. I don't remember getting into my sleeping bag or falling asleep.

25

"I'M GOING IN."

woke up to a high sun the next day. I sat up quickly, surprised to find my shoes and socks on the floor beside me. Rubbing the sleep from my eyes, I wondered if I'd actually taken them off or if Daisy had. I quickly tugged them back on and headed straight to the master bedroom. The door was locked.

I frowned. *That's strange. Why would they lock me out?*

"You're not setting one toe into that room without eating," came Daisy's no-nonsense voice from the kitchen.

I turned to see she'd been working for a long time; before me lay a breakfast fit for any king. Three kinds of muffins, two kinds of cereal, milk, orange, grape, and apple juice, several bananas, toast, and a whole hoard of other things, such as bacon and eggs.

"Wow! Expecting an army?" I teased, coming toward her.

"I'm expecting one ravenous boy to sit down right here," she pointed to a chair, "and eat up at least half this food, or he's not going into the field base."

"Come on, Daisy!" I protested. "I can eat while I work. A kid's been kidnapped!"

"And a kid's starving himself to find that kidnapped kid. Ace is in there working; he can handle things a little longer while you eat." Knowing I had less than no choice, I complied. "And don't even think about gobbling."

I groaned. "You sound just like Mom used to."

She smiled softly. I didn't talk about my parents much; it always pleased her when I did. "She knew her stuff. You'll be sick as any dog if you wolf down your food. Besides, you can do something no other person can to help with this case while you're eating."

My eyes lit up. "Now we're talking. What?"

"Dish up, then I'll tell."

It took a lot of self-control to move at a moderate speed. Finally, I had piled my plate full enough to satisfy Daisy.

"That will do for your first helping," she decided. I rolled my eyes. How much food did she think I could force inside me?

"Now, what's this thing only I can do?" I asked after a quick prayer, including asking protection over Philip and a fast return.

Daisy sat beside me and began peeling a banana to eat over her cinnamon muffin. "I know twins transmit feelings sometimes. You've told me you've felt what Philip has and vice versa, so I was thinking maybe Philip transmitted feelings to you."

I paused in buttering my blueberry muffin. "I, I don't know. I haven't noticed."

"I want you to try. See if you feel anything Philip might be feeling. Okay?"

I shrugged. "It's worth a shot. What's the use of having a twin if he can't get you out of trouble?" She smiled and patted my arm.

I sat there for several minutes, trying to define what I was really feeling and what Philip may be transmitting. The results frightened me. I continued to sit there, trying to be still so I could concentrate, and trying to eat to keep Daisy happy.

"Anything?"

I shook my head. "No. Nothing at all."

She sighed. "Maybe it needs more time. After all, you only just met a few months ago. Twins have all their lives to form bonds." She left to check on Ace and bring him a muffin and juice.

I remained sitting there. I knew what Daisy didn't—Philip and I had been transmitting feelings distantly since birth; that had only gotten stronger since meeting. I would have been able to feel something if he was transmitting.

That's what frightened me. Since meeting, a warm feeling had replaced the ache I'd always had for my twin. I'd figured out it meant I had a living brother out there. Now I didn't have that warm feeling or sense of another person. All I had was blankness. A black, empty void. It was as if Philip just ... *wasn't* anymore.

Ace and Daisy had been right, as usual, about making me sleep for a few hours. When I walked into the field base, it was as if it were a new situation entirely. I could think much clearer today, and I felt more distant than I'd been yesterday—which was a good thing. Yesterday, I'd been looking for my twin. Today, I was looking for Philip Taylor. I could do this without being emotionally attached—another good thing.

"What's happening?" I asked, taking a seat beside Ace on the bed.

"Nothing. All night we've kept the wires hot, but nothing's changed."

"Maybe it's time to take a different angle," I decided and turned away. I went into the living room and dropped onto the couch. Quickly, I pulled out my cellphone and started making calls. The first person I talked to was Henry. He gave me all the negatives about the campsite and the happenings. The last thing he said was we'd never see Philip alive again; I was determined to prove him wrong.

After Henry, I called Steve. As predicted, he gave me all the positives. The last thing he said was not to worry; we'd find Philip.

Lastly, I made the call I wasn't relishing. Allis didn't answer his phone; his bodyguard did. Before I could even speak with Allis, I had to give out a list of answers to who I was and how I knew Allis. The Billsons were definitely going to long lengths to keep Allis safe.

Finally, when I got to speak with Allis, I was shocked to find him civil. He apologized for the grilling, then asked me how I was doing with Philip missing. I told him I could be better, then asked him to tell me about the camping trip. Again, he surprised me. He told me everything he could remember, down to what clothes Philip was last seen wearing. Then he told me his biggest secret was reading Sherlock Holmes novels. He told me there had been no signs anywhere "the game was afoot." He said things had been as they'd always been before; there had been nothing to give warning to the kidnapping.

I asked him where the campsite was exactly—they'd wanted to surprise me, so I hadn't been told. Allis said it was near Lack Michigan, about two miles hike inland following a stream. I asked him next if it was a secluded spot, wondering how easy it had been for the kidnapper to find the boys.

Allis said it was secluded, but if you followed the stream, you couldn't miss it. The boys had built a fire pit and put up rope swings where the stream was deeper. It looked like a kid's campsite.

After a few minutes longer, I thanked him, told him not to worry about being kidnapped, then said goodbye.

As I hung up, Daisy came in. "Find anything?"

"Not sure. Henry told me the mosquitoes were as bad as always. Steve told me it had been peaceful and quiet, and the frogs had sung them to sleep at night. Allis says anyone who followed the stream would be able to find the campsite." I smiled a little. "Allis did turn out to be helpful. He told me what Philip was wearing last—down to the color of his socks."

"That was observant."

"It might help. Send this information to all the guys." I tore out the description of Philip that Allis had given me. "And start thinking of something to tell the Taylors as to why you sent me away."

She stopped short. Turning around, she said, "Excuse me?"

I pulled my backpack from my suitcase. "I'm going in."

26
ON THE HUNT

"You're what?"

I didn't look up from packing a few things into the bag. "I'm going in. To find Philip. I'm going to go to the campsite and work my way from there."

"You can't do that, Jesse. He's your twin—you're liable to get too emotional and take unnecessary risks."

"There's no choice." I stopped and looked up at her seriously. "Daisy, Philip and I aren't communicating. All I have is this *void* where he used to be. *I'm going in.*"

She stared at me as the implications sunk in. "You think he's dead."

"Or dying."

She was silent. I heard her draw in a deep breath and let it out slowly. "You're going to need a chopper to fly you out there. I'll get right on that."

I smiled. I knew she'd understand.

I boarded an unmarked CIA chopper twenty minutes later. The pilot was an old friend of my Mom's; he'd done missions with me before.

"Where to, Agent Best?" he called over the noise.

"Michigan! Northwest side of Lake Michigan!"

We took off. I waved goodbye to Daisy and Ace, who'd dropped me off at the private airstrip. We'd be in touch. They would send me everything new on the case, and I'd send them everything I found.

I parachuted from the helicopter under cover of darkness. Actually, that's when we arrived; I wanted to keep my coming a secret, so I'd rejected landing and opted to parachute. It wouldn't be the first time.

When I was safely on the ground, I waved a light stick, signaling it was okay for him to leave. He flashed his light once then turned back the way we'd come.

Drawing in a deep breath, I turned toward the woods. Allis said the trail wasn't obvious until five yards in; I'd find it by the directions Steve gave me.

Using night-vision goggles, I followed Steve's sketchy directions. After finding the trail, things went smoothly and quickly. All the baggage I had was a light backpack—all my other equipment was on me. I wore a repelling cord for a belt, and my wristbands were really grenades, just in case I had to blow my way into something. My shirt and pants contained secret compartments carrying things I'd need for communication. On my person were four guns—one in a shoulder holster, one in a back holster, and the other on my hip. The last one was more of a derringer than a gun, and it was strapped to the back of my calf. I was ready for a fight. I was expecting one, too.

I made my way deeper into the woods until finding the campsite just as the boys had described it. I went to work right away, looking for anything an untrained eye would miss. By tomorrow, I knew there would be a team of men hired to find Philip here, so I had no time to spare.

I combed the place over once, looking for footprints. Then a second time, looking for fibers of hair, blood, skin, or threads from snagged clothing. I couldn't find anything. I combed the place a third time with a special high-tech gadget that would give me the DNA of anyone who'd been there.

After combing, I began to think this was something much bigger than a ransom grab. I could only find DNA for three people. I looked everywhere, even widening my search, but only three people's DNA showed up.

Sitting down on a stump, I pondered this. There should have been at least four different types of DNA—five, counting the kidnapper. This bothered me. How could two DNA just disappear?

I pulled out my notebook and pen and began to write.

No signs of footprints other than those belonging to the boys
No fibers at all
Three types of DNA, one or two missing
How could the DNA be erased?
Who knows how to erase it?

I stopped to think. Who knew how to erase it? If I figured that out, I'd figure out a huge piece of the puzzle. I knew without a doubt that whoever was behind this was smart. Only smart men could pull this off without leaving any traces or anything that would be picked up on and followed.

I sat up a little straighter; my heart began to beat faster in my chest. I pulled my cellphone from its holder on my belt and the long-range transmitter from the compartment in my shoe. Quickly, I set up a phone call to Daisy.

The phone rang several times. Maybe Daisy and Ace were out playing the roles of Floor Parents. I was about to hang up when the call went through. "Hello? Jesse?" came Daisy's panting voice—she must have run to get the phone.

"Yes, and I have some news that could prove fatal." Quickly, I told her about the lack of DNA and the clean-swiped kidnapping. "It's way too professional to be a two-bit hood. There's a brain backing this kidnapping—brains and proficiency."

"Have any ideas?"

"Yeah, but it isn't pretty or neat. I messed up *somewhere,* and *someone* saw my face. See if anything is posted about Jesse Best going down."

"Do you think Philip was kidnapped on your behalf?"

"I don't know, really. The people I go up against have the brains and proficiency. They have a huge motive other than ransom, too."

"That explains why there's been no note."

"Yeah. Philip will die unless we find him in time—if he isn't dead already."

"And you think he is."

I sighed deeply. "I hope not, but I'm getting more and more convinced he is. Especially now."

"I'll get on it right away. You just be careful and promise not to do anything you wouldn't normally do."

"I promise." After a pause, I added, "Hey, don't get overly worried about this, Daisy. I may be wrong about who kidnapped Philip."

"Okay. Be careful, okay?"

"I will." I hung up the phone.

I paused only long enough to take a one-hour nap; Daisy was right about me needing my strength. After waking, I continued combing the woods. I walked in a widening circle around the campsite, hoping to pick up something to indicate in which direction they had taken Philip.

It was the break of dawn when things finally started looking up. I found traces of three people's DNA, and one matched Philip's. I called Daisy and let her know what I'd found and where I'd found it. Then I asked if she'd had any luck on her end.

"I've sent out feelers and spies all over, but nobody seems to be bragging."

"Has anything come back on the *Bliss'* guy?"

"Nothing."

"Keep working on him. I have this feeling that finding out who he is will bust this case wide open." I hung up and kept walking in the direction the DNA had pointed. Soon, I found more traces of DNA. They were getting fresher, too. I kept my eyes open for any traps. If I were the one kidnapping a famous detective/secret agent, I knew I'd cover my tracks with traps.

As though on cue, I heard a click. I froze, closing my eyes at my own stupidity. I had just stepped on a mine.

"Brilliant, Agent *Best*. Nice going, Detective *Best*. Wouldn't your parents be proud to see you now?" I belittled myself angrily. I had just finished thinking about traps and stepped on one! How stupid could I get? "Maybe I should change my name to *Loser*."

I couldn't chew myself out now—I had to get out of this. Carefully, I looked down. At first glance, the little tree by the tip of my toe looked as if it'd been growing there for months. However, after careful examination, I saw it wasn't a tree at all— it was a new growth of a tree branch. Someone had picked it up and stuck it into the ground to warn fellow members of the mine, no doubt. Anyone who didn't know the tree was a marker would have done what I'd done. If they hadn't been listening, they'd have been blown up.

"Very clever." I applauded my opponent. "You win round one, but not the whole game." Carefully, I crouched down. Using a small hand mirror, I saw how the bomb was set up. With extreme caution, I used tools I carried in pouches in my clothing to disarm the mine.

Drawing in the first real breath since stepping on the explosive, I took my foot from the trigger. I'd have to remember to keep my eyes open for tree markers from now on—along with anything else.

Before moving on, I picked up the miniature bomb and examined it. It wasn't like other mines I'd dealt with. This one was different, with its own unique design, as though someone had made it themselves and not bought it from a manufacturer. The make and style looked familiar. I was sure I'd seen it before but couldn't place it.

Quickly, I took some digital pictures and sent them to Daisy, along with the message to check out the bomb and see if it matched anyone's records. I also told her to send anonymous tips to any crime fighters searching for Philip to be on the lookout for the tree markers and mines.

I continued with extreme caution, scanning the ground and trees around me. If anything looked remotely like a mine, I stopped and checked it out, and if it proved to be a bomb, I disarmed it. Even with time being crucial, I couldn't leave the mines behind for some innocent person to step on.

The DNA I was following was getting stronger by the minute. It was eerie in a way, almost as though some kind of chemical had been sprayed to wipe out or confuse the DNA, and now it was fading away little by little. Soon, I'd be able to send the DNA I was getting to Daisy, who'd try to find a match. Things were really starting to look up.

At 10:30, things turned from black to gray. I was walking along, eyes wide for mines, when a stab of pain hit my right arm.

Thinking I'd walked into a trap, I hurled myself backward. I landed on my stomach, gun drawn, ready to blow whatever had hit me into smithereens. Nothing happened—no follow-up, no continued fire, nothing at all.

Frowning, I looked around. All was normal; even the birds were chirping. I lay there for several more minutes, trying to figure out what had happened. Slowly, I moved to check how bad my arm was hurt. There was no blood—that was a good thing. I carefully pulled up my sleeve and studied my arm. There wasn't even a mark.

Suddenly, I felt another jab of pain, this time on my leg. Rolling to cover, I checked for damage. Again, there was nothing there.

Wait a second, I thought suspiciously. *If there are no marks and nothing here to hit me, how am I being hit?* Suddenly, I felt very foolish. Here I was, diving around the woods, and it wasn't *me* who was getting hit—it was Philip!

"Philip!" I sat bolt upright as the truth sunk in. "Of course— he's transmitting. But if he's transmitting, he can't be dead. Who would hit a corpse, and how would it transmit?" I whooped in triumph. My twin wasn't dead! I had more time.

"Hang in there, Philip," I said, hoping to transmit my feelings to him. "I'm on my way."

I grabbed my cellphone and long-distance transmitter. A few moments later, I was talking to Ace. "We're looking for a boy, Ace, not a body! Philip's transmitting to me again. He's not dead."

"Praise the Lord! That is something to be thankful for."

"Yeah, I just wish he wasn't transmitting so hard," I complained, rubbing my throbbing side. "He's getting a hard beating, and it's like I'm getting hit, too."

"Are you all right?"

"Sure—Philip's the one who's in trouble. I'm guessing he was under heavy drugs to be easier to handle. Now that the drug has worn off, he's 'alive' again. That's all I can think of at the moment."

"Sounds logical. Anything else happen since you last called?"

"Nothing."

"We ran those mines."

I perked up. "What'd you get?"

"They resemble some that were used a couple of years ago in a bombing, only those were much bigger."

I took out my pen and notebook. "Who was behind the bombing?"

"Ready for another letdown? The bombers were never apprehended. No one knows for sure what the reason behind the bombing was, or who the brains behind it were."

"What was bombed?"

"An empty Catholic church."

I quirked an eyebrow. "What?"

"You heard right."

"Why would anyone bomb *that?*"

"Only the bombers know."

"Was I or my parents connected to that church or the case?"

"No. It was before you were on active duty, and your parents had nothing to do with it. Why?"

"I've come in contact with these mines before, I know it. The time, date, and enemy are all evading me. Wouldn't you know it? Everything seems to be against us on this one."

"You're not the only one with that feeling. The guys who were hired to find Philip are saying the same thing. You better watch out—they'll be trailing you, and since they don't have any mines to dodge, they'll be going faster than you. Besides, they don't know a detective/agent is the one thought to be kidnapped. They won't be looking for things like you have been."

"Thanks for the heads up. I'll watch out."

"Okay. I'll call you when something new comes in."

"Gotcha." I hung up.

"Okay, Best, let's see if you really are the best," I said aloud. "What do a Catholic church bombing and a kidnapping have in common? Philip's not Catholic, so religion can't be it. Catholic churches are rich, and the Taylors are rich, but no money was demanded in both cases. Could the bomb maker and mine maker in this case have sold the explosives to the bomber and kidnapper? If so, there doesn't have to be any connection at all. Except the explosives maker."

I sighed. This puzzle was annoying; there were too many twists and quirks and not enough straights and normal.

27

BREAKTHROUGH

I was breaking for lunch when the phone buzzed. I picked it up quickly. "Best."

"Jesse, we got a break!" Ace said excitedly. "Daisy's calling all units with the information now."

"What is it?"

"You know the guy at *Bliss*? We finally have a name for him—Devlin O'Brian. He's a man working in a terrorist group thought to have been wiped out a year ago. He and several others have apparently been in hiding ever since, but now there's activity in the old hideout again."

My eyes widened as things that had been evading me suddenly came forward with a bang. "Ace, last year, April 12th, I was in Ireland tracking a bunch of terrorists. I came across landmines marked with stones to match the terrain! It's just like here, except they used tree branches."

"And Devlin O'Brian is Irish *and* a terrorist. I think you're getting this, Jess."

"Another piece of the puzzle just fell in. The *Huszars* especially liked to target religions, and you told me bombs like these mines were used to blow up a Catholic church. That fits their profile. They have a huge motive: I was the one who brought them to justice."

"We thought we'd gotten them all," Ace agreed grimly. "One of them must have slipped away after seeing your face."

"They're seeking revenge, but they're going to take it out on Philip." I sprang to my feet. "Ace, how soon can you get a two-propeller plane up here to pick me up?"

"A two-propeller plane?"

"They're faster than choppers and can take me right over to Ireland."

"Wait a second—you don't have clearance to go."

"You can get it for me while I'm in the air."

"I could, sure, but—"

"Ace, come on," I interrupted, packing up my lunch and starting to jog back to the clearing where I'd meet the plane. "We have to get someone in that terrorist camp now, and there's no one that knows it better than me. You can't refute that."

"I know that, but it's you who they're after."

"And it's my identical twin who they have."

"But, how do you plan to get in?"

I grinned. "Same way I got in last time."

"Walking right up to the terrorists' base, then snaking your way in, hoping you won't get caught?"

"It worked."

I heard him sigh. "But what's this about a two-propeller plane? How can you expect it to land?" I told him my plan. "You're crazy, Agent Best." I could hear his grin. "Just like your parents."

I smiled fondly. "I *am* their son."

"Not to mention the best. Okay, I'll have a plane waiting for you in half an hour. Does that give you enough time?"

I checked my watch. "Plenty."

Exactly thirty minutes later, I stood at the edge of the woods, watching for my ticket to Ireland. I heard it coming from the east and turned to watch its approach. It came just as I'd requested, flying low over the treetops, cargo hatch open.

It passed over Lake Michigan once, just as it was supposed to. Then it banked left for a return pass. Just as it cleared the trees on the south side, a rope ladder tumbled down from its open cargo hold.

I waited, timing the exact instant to run out from the trees. *Five, four, three, two, one—go!* I shot from my cover right before the plane passed. I made it just in time to grab the swinging ladder with my right hand. I winced as my shoulder took the whole of my weight when the ground fell away as the craft began to climb higher.

Taking a deep breath, I began to climb up the precariously swinging ladder. Up and up I went, thinking about how high off the ground I was. If I slipped and fell, it was a straight shot into Heaven.

But I didn't slip. I made it all the way up the ladder and grabbed the hand reaching out for mine. I was hauled into the hold and the door shut behind me safely. Breathing hard, I rubbed my sore shoulder—it'd taken the brunt of the ride. Again.

"Jesse Best. I should have known a stunt like this came out from your sleeve."

I looked up at the young man who'd helped me into the craft. "Bruce! I thought you'd gone into something less dangerous than flying for the CIA."

My old daredevil pal shrugged. "Got bored. Charter flights weren't half as exciting as picking up my little pal in the most creative ways."

"If I'd known you were up here waiting for me," I shot back, "I'd have thought up something better."

He chuckled. "I bet you would have." He leaned closer to me as though about to tell a huge secret. "And if I'd have known who it was I'd be picking up, first I'd have never come, and second I'd have given the ladder a few hard tugs."

"It's great to see you again, Bruce."

"It's great to see you too, Jesse.... So, where are we heading?" he asked, leading the way forward to where the others waited. "Knowing you the way I do, I'd guess it's not on vacation."

"Hah, you could wish. We're on our way to Ireland for a snatch/grab operation against terrorists."

He clicked his tongue. "Now, you see? This is why I quit the CIA in the first place. Every time I get near you, I nearly get my head shot off by terrorists."

"Hey, that scrape in North Korea was not my fault."

"Ne-ver."

I punched his shoulder.

He chuckled and pulled open the door separating the cargo hold and the passenger lounge, which was full of CIA men and PJs. "Hey, boys!" Bruce called, getting everyone's attention. "Guess who we get stuck with? The kid agent who likes to kill off his teammates! Gentlemen," he pulled me into the lounge, "welcome Agent Jesse Best." Over exaggerated groans filled the cabin.

"Oh, no!" a tall man cried in mock dread. "Not him again!"

"Where we get to go down this time, Best?" a bearded man asked. "Cuba?"

I grinned back at the familiar faces. "Nothing quite so bad— just Ireland."

"Belfast?"

I shot him a mischievous grin. "How'd you guess?"

"Boys," the bearded man, Anthony, warned, looking around. "Get ready for the machineguns. Best is with us again, and you all know what that means."

Several mocking statements such as, "If I don't get out alive this time, send these letters to my folks and wife" filled the cabin. I just grinned and took a seat beside Bruce.

I'd worked with all these men before, on the same mission. It was the North Korean job where we'd been blown out of the sky and had to trek our way out, with enemies looking for us all over. Of course, because I was the kid, I got all the blame for it—all in fun, you understand. Everyone knows it wasn't really my fault, but it's a lasting complaint whenever we get together.

"So, Jesse, what's it gonna be this time?" Bob asked, leaning down against my seat.

"Oh, you know me, Bob. Whenever I go near Ireland, I'm only after one thing."

"Terrorists," all the men announced.

"Hey, you said something about a snatch/grab back in the cargo hold," Bruce reminded me. "Who's been nabbed?"

I smiled softly. They'd never believe me if I told them the truth, so I simply said, "A millionaire's son named Philip Taylor."

"Oh, I've heard of him," Yule announced. "It's all over the networks. Who in Belfast kidnapped him? They're saying it was a clean swipe kidnapping."

"The cleanest. They made a few mistakes, though. One, letting me see one of the guys sent to stalk Taylor. Two, deploying mines only used by this certain group to wipe out any followers. Three, nabbing a kid who's close to me."

"Ouch. That last one will cost them. Who're the lucky terrorists about to have you breathing down their necks?"

"The *Huszars*."

"But you wiped them out last year."

"That's what we thought, too. Apparently, they had a few men who escaped and now are back in business. At least, that's what I'm supposed to be checking out. There's been reported activity in the old base. I'm going to drop in like last time and see if I can find Taylor."

"No wonder we got elected for this run—we dropped you the last time."

"—and nearly got blown to bits picking you up."

"Now you get a second chance to erase that mark. I'll need you to stick around and pick me up, and hopefully, Taylor."

"I knew this was coming."

"Do us a favor, Jesse," Ned begged. "Try to disarm the air guns. We want to live a few minutes longer."

I grinned. "I'll do my ... *best*."

Darkness was a worldwide synonym with evil, but it held a lot of good in it, too. I used it regularly on this case. At exactly two minutes to midnight, the CIA two-propeller plane circled over the *Huzsars'* base. The guys were all at their stations, looking for signs of life; they didn't want to drop me into this bombsite if there weren't any people.

"I'm picking up human activity all over the place," Ned reported, eyes glued to the screen before him.

"Riley, any conversation going on?" Bruce asked as he went over my gear again. Ever since an accident he and I had been in while parachuting, Bruce always checked me over three times.

"Affirmative," he replied, holding his hand over his headphone. "At least four men are talking about a bomb they're making, and several others are in the main hall. They're talking about their prisoner."

I looked up. *Will they say they have Jesse Best, and things will turn upside down?* I knew things would get interesting for the guys when they picked me up again, but I had no time to tell them the story now. Once Philip was safe in the air, I'd fill them in.

"Are they saying anything about their hostage?"

"Not that I can tell. It does sound like two or three people are in that tiny shed they used to keep guns in. They're not saying anything, though. Wait a minute! It's where they have the boy! They just spoke to him, and he's groaning. Judging by the sounds, they're treating him rough."

I bit my lip as a stab of pain tore through my ribs. I rubbed the pain away; they were really working him over. I had no idea how I was going to make this up to him.

"What's with that?" I nearly jumped at Bruce's words. He was frowning at me. "Are you hurt?"

"Not really."

"You sure you don't want me to come with you?"

"No, it's better for one."

"Positive?" I nodded. "Then are you ready?"

I nodded again. "There's only one more thing you have to know."

"What's that?" Yule raised a suspicious eyebrow.

"The pickup plan. Swing by in fifteen minutes exactly. If I'm not there, come back around in five minutes. If I'm still not there, go home." I tugged my infrared goggles over my eyes. "That's an order—we aren't having another mission like the last one."

"Who will pick you up, then?"

"I'll trek out. When it's safe, I'll call."

"Yes, sir, Best."

"We're over the site," the pilot said over the intercom.

"Open the hatch, Bruce." Bruce threw the lever, and the door opened. Offering a salute, I apologized, "You'll have to excuse me," and jumped from the plane.

28

DANGEROUS MISSION

landed on the grass fifty yards from the terrorist base. Brushing myself off, I removed the parachute. Looking through the night vision goggles, I surveyed my surroundings, deciding the best way in. While on the plane, I'd changed into all black and camouflaged my face with paint. I'd be able to slip in and out in less than fifteen minutes—without detection if all went right.

Glancing at my watch, I saw I had thirteen minutes before the pick-up pass. The shed I had to get to was on the other side, past the main hall and the bomb-building room. I needed to get going.

Taking a pose as though I had every right to be there, I boldly walked toward the first building. My dad taught me this when I was ten. He'd said, "Sneaking around works well in some cases, but in others, it's better to act like you belong. Take rescue missions, for instance. If you walk around the camp like a sentry in the dark of night, chances are, nobody will challenge you, thinking you're with them." I'd practiced that many times. Most of the time, it worked.

I looked around for a real lookout once I got to the first building. I spied him high up in the tower on the west corner. Smiling to myself, I kept walking; they were using the same defense they'd used a year ago. And why not? It worked for years before that. Another guard was in the south tower, and so on until all corners were covered. A few others were stationed below ground with a periscope, but Ned was taking care of them. He'd scramble their mechanism, so they'd always read clear. I could stand right in front of one and never be seen.

Even with all this, I moved with great care; this mission was too important to make mistakes. Too many people depended on me: Philip, the guys on the plane, people these terrorists would attack in the future if not stopped, lastly, my own life.

"Do us a favor, Jesse. Try to disarm the air guns. We want to live a few minutes longer."

Ned's words floated to me as I crouched beside a shed used to store scrap metal for bombs. Disarm the air guns. I needed to do that before taking on the men in the shed with Philip.

I sharply changed direction and silently sped toward the air control room I'd learned of last time. Cautiously, I peeked through the window to see who and how many were inside— three beefy men. I sank back down, leaning my back against the wall.

I really didn't want to alert them to my presence by knocking out any of the men on duty, yet I had to disarm those guns. I thought over the dilemma, pulling out a small magnet, a tracking device, a couple of wires, and other miscellaneous items.

When most kids were five, they were watching *Barney*— not me. I'd never watched normal kids' shows or cartoons. My movie times had been shows like *MacGyver* or other agent things.

I'd learned a lot from them and the lessons and tests taken from them.

Now I worked on something I knew MacGyver would have been proud of. Three minutes later, I placed the magnet against the metal door near the handle. Attached to the magnet was the tiny tracking device that would now scramble the air guns, making them completely useless. I grinned as I remembered Mom's excitement at seeing my first homemade scrambler. We'd gotten pizza and ice cream to celebrate; I'd been six.

Rechecking my watch, I saw only seven minutes remained before the first pass. I wanted to make that rendezvous. I pushed off the wall and raced toward the shed.

I was only a few feet away when the door burst open, showering the night with light and filling the air with curses. I dove for the side of the shed and rolled behind it. Breathing raggedly, I sat up, back against the wall for support.

"Stupid boy," one man growled. He followed it with fierce Irish curses.

"Leave him be 'til Devlin comes—he wants to kill him himself for the setbacks."

"Do you think the CIA knows who took Best?" The first man asked as they slammed the door and began to walk toward the main base.

"They're not stupid, O'Hara. They'll be here when they figure out everything, but it won't be until we're gone. Only Best could have linked the mines to us, and he's here. We have enough time to kill him and pack up."

"You know, maybe we should call Best 'Worst' from now on— he really messed this one up. Nothing like he was last time. You know he didn't even fight us?"

"Like we gave him the chance?" Their fading laughter was the last I heard from them.

So, they plan to move after killing me, I thought, as I waited a moment before making my move. *They're only here because this is where they were busted, and they wanted me to die here.*

Sober thought; it would complicate things. I had to get agents here before they got away. Swishing air around in my mouth, I decided to change plans. It wasn't normal to change plans in the middle of the action, but this time, it might be the only way to get them all for good.

I pressed the emergency backup button on my watch. On the plane, Yule would get the message, and they'd think I needed help; choppers would be here in a few minutes. I'd explain everything to the guys once the terrorists were locked up.

Knowing I had to get out of here before the wrap-up started, I dashed around the corner, looked around, saw no one, and then crept to the door. I grabbed the doorknob with a gloved hand and shoved it opened.

I dove in, hitting the ground rolling, then springing to my feet, a gun in each hand. I scanned the room with my eyes; only Philip was inside. He stared up at me, eyes wide and fearful. He was chained to the ground spread eagle, but there was nothing to keep him from screaming.

"Keep silent, and we'll get out of here alive," I commanded, dropping by his side. "I'm agent Best, and I'm here to rescue you." I had disguised my voice, making it deeper, older. He wouldn't recognize me, but even as I worked to keep him from knowing who I was, I knew I would have to tell him or go crazy with guilt.

"Not now," I muttered. I took out my skeleton keys and began jimmying the locks.

"Where'd you come from?" Philip's voice was raspy and barely audible.

I laid a gentle hand over his cracked lips. "Silence, Philip Taylor. Silence is survival." I quoted my Dad's words. Philip closed his eyes and relaxed against the hard floor, or maybe he was just too exhausted to fight any longer.

I looked him over behind dark glasses as I worked. He wasn't half as bad as I'd feared, but I could see ugly bruises all over. His lips were puffy and bleeding, as was his nose. There were ugly cuts here and there, and I could tell he hadn't eaten or drank since his abduction. *I'll make it up to you, Brother. I promise.*

The locks loudly clicked as they popped opened to free him. I looked at his chafed wrists; he'd tried to pull free some time during his imprisonment.

Philip opened his swollen eyes and looked down at his freed wrists. He tried to sit up but was too weak. He moaned.

"You'll be out of here soon, Taylor, back with your parents where you belong," I told him as I pulled him to his feet. His legs buckled beneath him, but I wouldn't let him fall. "Slip your arm around my shoulders, and I'll help you out of here." He stiffly obeyed.

I wished there had been more time so I could massage away the stiffness, but we were cutting it close as it was. Slowly, I dragged him toward the door. He tried to help but was unable.

With one of Philip's arms around my shoulders, I peeked out; no one in sight. I was about to open the door and slip out when a near-fatal error hit me hard enough to knock my breath out. The light! It had poured from the door when the men walked out. It would have poured from the door when I dove in. Any one of the lookouts would have seen it and sounded the alarm.

"Oh, boy," I muttered. I was going to have to change plans *again*. This case was certainly going to be written down—if I survived.

Thinking fast, heart beating even faster, I lowered Philip to the ground and whirled to the other side of the cabin. I checked my inventory for the fastest way out of this cabin. The laser looked like my best tool. I grabbed the pen-sized laser and aimed it at the lightbulb. After it shattered, pitching us into darkness, I went to work cutting a door from the shed wall.

I thought about how much time I had to get us out of here as I worked. If they really had seen the light, they'd be here in a matter of seconds—a minute at the most. I was running too low. We'd never get out of this building before they came.

We haven't got a choice. If we stray here and try to make a stand, they'll blow up the building. We have to get out. Finishing the door, I turned off my laser then rushed to Philip's side. He was sitting up on his own, rubbing his aching limbs.

"Gimme your hand," I ordered. He held it out to me, and I grabbed it, pulling him up again. Just as I kicked the door open, I heard pounding feet coming from the other direction. They were here.

If only Philip could run! Then we'd have a better chance. *Almighty God, get us out of here, please,* I desperately prayed as I pulled Philip over my shoulder fireman style and began to run as fast as I could into the night.

The air was filled with savage cursing behind me. Orders were given, and men ran to carry them out. The roars of engines coming to life made my throat dry. I knew I couldn't out-run them on motorcycles. I wildly looked around for a place to make a stand until help came.

The dugout—I remembered it from last time; it was the gang's strongest defense point. It could even withstand bombings. I prayed with all my might we'd get there before they ran us down.

We didn't.

I was jumping the wide gully separating me from the clearing the dugout stood in when a bullet tore through my shirt. I landed the flying leap on the opposite side of the gully and quickly slid down into it. It was better than lying out in the open.

Instinct had me going for my guns even before I stopped rolling. Philip yelped as he struck the ground. Whimpering, he pressed his face into my back. The motorcyclist roared over the gully, momentarily blinding me with its brake lights.

Sightless, I fired at the sound. I heard a scream of pain mixed with terror, then the sound of a crash. I'd hit him, and he'd lost control.

Philip sobbed against me. In a weak moment, I bitterly wondered if I had ever been so lucky as to be afraid instead of the one needing to be cool.

I untangled myself from Philip slowly. I had to think fast. I was pinned down with more motorists coming at me from every direction. How could I get Philip out of here, or at least out of immediate danger?

The thought agonized me. "Stay here and low," I ordered in Philip's ear. The best I could do was make a diversion. I ran crouched along the gully ten paces. Looking back at him, I saw he'd curled up into as small a shape as possible.

I fired at the sounds around me. I didn't expect to hit anything, I just wanted to give them a new target to shoot at. If they thought Philip was over here, they wouldn't stay where he truly was.

As I lay on my back waiting for a move, I heard motors changing directions to come to me. In a split second, lights from twelve different motorcycles were aimed at the spot above my head. I heard muffled orders yelled and tightened my grip on my guns.

A hand grenade fell to the ground five feet to my left. I flipped to my stomach, then onto my knees and dove as far as I could to the right, closer to Philip. Behind me, the grenade blew up. I covered my head as chunks of earth rained down on me.

The bomb hadn't been intended to get me—it was only to keep me ducked while four men rushed the gully. They dove down, guns spitting fire. Earth kicked up all around me. I raised my guns and returned fire.

While they ducked for cover, I scrambled backward. Philip would need someone to cover him if they were coming down to meet my bullets. A gun fired. A second later, a bullet chewed into the ground between my thumb and pointer. I jerked my hand back and fired at the man I saw about to fire again.

Things were getting dirty. They had night vision goggles, too; it was only a matter of seconds before they saw Philip and me and blew us to bits. Moving desperately, I continued firing with my right hand to keep them down a few seconds more while I searched for my bright light with my left.

I shoved my goggles back, briefly plunging me into blackness. Then my fingers found the button I was seeking and pushed it. Light as bright as the sun filled the gully as the four men screamed in pain. Blindly, they ran down the gully, tearing their goggles off.

I flipped off the light but didn't dare put my goggles back on. If they used the same trick on me, I would be just like those four men. Instead, I moved backward until my foot touched Philip.

Philip had been huddling in a ball. I touched his side, and he jumped two feet in the air in fright. This actually saved his life. While I'd been taking out the men to my left, four others had been sneaking up on my right. One had just gotten a bead on Philip when he jumped; the bullet went beneath him.

I whirled and dropped two of them at the sound, forcing the other two out of the gully. Philip whimpered as he looked at the dead men—the first he'd ever seen. I turned away from them; I'd deal with it later. I hated killing, but it wasn't possible to do anything less sometimes, not if I wanted to survive.

"Philip, we have to move—now!" I ordered over the constant commotion of gunfire and engines. "Crawl back that way." I pointed toward my right. "I'll keep them busy while you make an escape."

Philip didn't obey; he was staring at me unbelievingly. That's when I realized I hadn't dropped my voice, and I'd called him Philip. Topping that, my face was clearly visible; he knew it was me.

Piercing my lips at my huge blunder, I shoved him to the ground and covered him with my body just as another grenade blew a gaping hole only a few feet above us.

"Jesse. Jesse," Philip murmured into my ear.

"Don't say a word—not even my name," I growled. I rolled off him and waited for the next volley of grenades or bullets. Instead, I heard the sound of a helicopter. I felt like whooping with joy—my backup had come, and in time.

"That's our ticket home, Philip!" I cried joyously. "You'll be back home in a short while; just hang on until then." Philip nodded, burying his face against my chest as five CIA choppers flew overhead. Spotlights turned the area into day as men repelled down all around us, shouting orders for the terrorists to surrender.

As the men above began wrapping up the terrorists, or what was left of them after our skirmish, I turned to Philip and directed, "Stay in the gully, Philip. I'm going to talk."

"Don't leave me alone."

"I'm not. I'm just going to talk. The man will come to me."

He did so as soon as I climbed out of the gully. "Looks like you took out most of them on your own, Agent Best," he praised, indicating the handful of men who remained—one of them, I noticed, was Devlin O'Brian. I guess he'd arrived before the confrontation started. That was good. At least this time, I knew we'd really rounded them all up.

The agent spoke to me again. "Where's the boy, Agent Best?"

"I told him to remain in the gully." I indicated the bodies scattered around the edge of the gully. "Not the ideal wallpaper, you know."

He nodded grimly. "We'll lower a sling and get him out of here."

Just then, my two-propeller flew overhead, flashing its lights.

"Never mind, Agent O'Malley—those guys are here to take Master Taylor and me home." I pulled out my walkie-talkie and made contact with Bruce.

"Man alive, Best! What happened down there?" Bruce's voice came booming over the speaker.

"Got dirty."

"Do you want to bring Taylor with us or hop on one of those choppers?"

"With you—you're equipped with medical stuff, and you're faster. Lower a sling, and I'll get him settled."

A minute later, a huge black sling dropped lightly to the ground. Attached to it were four lines that would pull us back up in a moment. While the plane circled us, I quickly pulled Philip from the gully, covering his eyes with my sunglasses so he couldn't see our surroundings easily. Actually, that was a good thing—nobody would see his face until I was ready.

I situated Philip in the middle of the sling, fastened straps over him, and wrapped a warm blanket around him. After that, I tugged on the rope, signaling they should bring us up. Just as the sling rose off the ground, I clipped a safety line to it that was attached to my belt. Together, Philip and I rose high off the ground.

Two minutes later, Bruce and Ned gently lowered the sling onto the plane's floor. I unclipped myself and knelt beside Philip. He was exhausted, and the rocking of the sling and warmth of the blanket had put him to sleep. I smiled—at least I wouldn't have to fill him in yet.

"What do you want?"

"An IV for starters," I replied, un-strapping the last fastening. "He's dehydrated."

In a matter of minutes, Philip was resting on a soft bed, an IV stuck in his hand. On the other side was a monitor. Philip still wore my glasses, and I didn't move to take them off.

Sitting beside him, I traced a finger across his dirty cheek. "He'd never seen a dead man before tonight."

Bruce squeezed my shoulder. "It's tough for all of us. None of us enjoy death."

"Is that why he's got those glasses on?" Ned wondered.

"Yeah. Two men were shot before his eyes—I didn't want him to see the gore around us."

"You sure like this kid. How well do you know him?" Ned reached over and began to pull the glasses off his face. I remained silent, knowing the second the glasses were gone, I'd be up to my neck in explanations.

Bruce and Ned gasped. They stared at Philip's sleeping face, then looked at me. Bruce was the first to speak. "Jesse, I don't understand."

"Philip Taylor is my identical twin brother. We only met a couple of months ago."

29
SHARING MY SECRET

"Jesse?"

I blinked my eyes open, turning to see Philip was awake. Smiling, I sat up straight. "Hey, Brother. How you feeling now?" I adjusted his IV.

He didn't answer; he had other things on his mind. "Was all that a dream? Did you really rescue me from those guys and call yourself Agent Best? Did that all really happen, or did I hit my head and dream it all?"

I pulled up the blanket, tucking it around his shoulders. "Don't excite yourself; you're weak."

He took my hand. "Please, tell me."

"Ten minutes till you jump, Best," Bruce said from the doorway before ducking back out.

Philip looked at me, openmouthed. "It's true, unless I'm still dreaming."

I took his hand. "Philip, please, I don't have time to tell you everything right now. Believe me, and don't say anything about what I did to anyone—not even your parents. I will tell you everything when I get the chance, but I can't right now."

"I don't understand."

"I know. I will tell you everything. I promise."

"Not a word to anybody?"

"No one. Better yet, don't say anything about your kidnapping until I get a chance to talk to you. It's really important."

"But... What do you want me to say?"

I grinned. "Thank you, Philip. Just say you don't want to talk about it right now. If you're asked how you got away, say the agent who rescued you will get in contact with your parents. Okay?"

"I guess so. But you will tell me, right?"

"Yes. Above all things, don't say you saw me. I'm supposed to be in a safe house in Miami."

"Best, we're over Miami."

"I have to go. Bruce will take care of you. You'll be back with your parents soon." I squeezed his hand again, then dashed out after Bruce.

That night, I got a phone call from Daisy telling me it was safe to come back. Twenty minutes later, I boarded a private jet and flew all the way home. I landed on the Taylors' own airstrip then was transported by golf cart to the mansion, where I was taken to the hospital where Philip had been admitted. The Taylors were waiting for me in Philip's room. Philip, thankfully, was sleeping.

"Hi," I whispered softly, taking a seat beside Mrs. Taylor.

"Oh, hello, Jesse—I'm so glad you're back." She took my hand and held it. "He's sleeping," she said, even though it was obvious.

"What do the doctors say? Is he badly hurt?"

"No. He has several cuts and bruises, but nothing that won't go away with time. He *is* dehydrated and needs to eat regularly."

"Did he say anything about what happened?"

Mr. Taylor shook his head. "He refuses to talk about it. He did say an agent would contact us, but not when or why."

I hid a smile.

Philip was released from the hospital a week later. I had a feeling he was going to be annoyed with me when he saw me; I had visited him only when I knew he'd be sleeping, as I hadn't wanted to talk at the hospital.

I was looking out for his arrival when the limo drew up to the front steps, and I bounded down them to greet him; I could do nothing less, or people would start to wonder. One of the employees lifted him out of the car and carried him to his bedroom, even though he protested he was strong enough to walk.

Once we reached our bedroom, Mr. Carpenter carried Philip to his bed. Mrs. Warren, the head housekeeper, puttered over him. "I'm fine, Mrs. Warren," he insisted. "You could get Jesse and me some cold banana milks, though."

The plump old lady beamed. "I'll be right back with them. I sort of guessed you would want your favorite power drink, so I fixed one for each of you already." She dashed out the door.

Philip turned to glare at me, but before he could speak, the head housekeeper returned. A younger maid was behind her, carrying the two drinks on a tray. Philip smiled. "Thanks Mrs. Warren and Mallory." They delivered the drinks right to our hands then left. Before they shut the door, Philip asked them to tell everyone that we didn't want to be disturbed.

The second their footsteps died away, Philip looked at me again. "Why didn't you visit me? I would have visited you."

I looked at him a second, then stopped drinking from my straw. "I did—"

"Only when I was asleep. You didn't stick around for me to wake up."

I sighed, setting the drink down. "I was scared you'd press me into talking. I couldn't explain with all those nurses so close by; it was too dangerous for us both. But I'll explain now if you're not too mad at me."

"I'm not really mad at you; I was just hurt you were never there."

"I wished I was. I never wanted to leave your side."

He smiled. "I know that—now.... Tell me everything. How did you do all that?"

I picked up my huge glass, twirling the contents in circles with a twist of my wrist. "We're going to need more of these. This will take quite some time...."

"Wow," Philip whispered when I'd finished telling him how I'd gotten to be who I was. "That's amazing."

I sipped my fifth banana milk. "It's also deadly important to keep it a secret. Only a handful of people know Jesse Target is Jesse Best."

"Wow. Now I've gotten to join their ranks! I feel so proud—of you, and that I get to know."

"Hold your pride for a few minutes while I confess something."

"What do you mean?"

I took a deep breath, tears filling my eyes. "Philip, I'm so sorry. It's all my fault you were kidnapped and treated like this. They thought you were me, and they were going to kill you because I ruined their operations last year. I'm so sorry. If I could have, I would have done everything to stop them."

He stared at me blankly a moment before speaking. "You mean they kidnapped me because they thought they were getting you?"

I nodded miserably. "That's why I had to rescue you myself. I couldn't live if you were killed on my behalf."

Now he looked hurt. "So, if I'd never been kidnapped, you'd never have trusted me enough to tell me about your secret life?"

I put a hand on his shoulder, longing for him to understand. "Philip, this isn't the movies where a kid becomes an agent, and he'll never get beaten or hurt—this is real life. It's dangerous for me, and now because I told you, for you, too. I didn't want to tell you because it puts you in danger. It had nothing to do with trust!"

"Then why are you suddenly telling me?"

"I couldn't live without having your forgiveness for being kidnapped in my place. I would have had it any other way if it kept you out of danger. I'm so sorry. I never intended this to happen, or I would have..." I groped for what I would have done. "Well, I would have done *something* to prevent you from going through that."

He was silent a long time before pushing my hand away. I was surprised by his reaction, but then he wrapped me in a tight hug. "I forgive you, Jesse. You feel horrible about what happened, but I feel honored I could be in your place. I know it's dangerous. I know this isn't the movies like you said, but I'll gladly bear the danger right alongside you because I love you. You're my brother, Jesse. I love you."

Slowly, I raised my arms from my sides to wrap around him. "I love you too, Philip."

A few minutes later, we pulled away from each other. Philip sniffed and rubbed his hand across his nose. "I guess I can't tell anyone, right?"

I grinned. "Raise your right hand." He did. "Now repeat after me. I, say your name."

"I, Philip Justin Taylor."

"Do solemnly swear in the presence of God and Agent Jesse Best."

"Do solemnly swear in the presence of God and Agent Jesse Best."

"Never to reveal the information invested in me."

"Never to reveal the information invested in me."

I dropped my hand. "Now you're under oath not to tell."

He dropped his hand too. "And I won't. Not to anyone."

I challenged, "Not even your parents?"

"Not even them."

"Good because I wouldn't want you to beat me to it."

He gasped happily. "You mean you're going to tell them?"

I nodded grimly. "I have to. I need their forgiveness, too, and I need to know what they'll want from me. I can't give up my secret life as Jesse Best—it would be like a death sentence, Philip." I hoped he'd understand.

He reached over and gave my hand a firm squeeze. I knew he did.

Several days later, when Philip was feeling better, he asked his parents to come into the library with him. He wanted to introduce them to a very special friend. They agreed and followed him.

We'd been planning how I would do this since I told Philip about my real life. We'd decided to tell them in the room of beginnings—our nickname for the library since that's where I'd first met them. I would be waiting and then tell them about my secret life.

I was hiding behind a bookshelf when Philip led them into the room and to a pair of chairs we'd placed by the fountain. I watched from behind books while Philip locked the door, much as I had my first time here. Then he walked over to stand before the seated adults. "Mom, Dad, allow me to intrude to you a boy who is very important to me. Friend," he called to me, motioning me to come out.

Taking a deep breath, I reminded myself I was the best, then stepped from behind the bookshelf. "Hello, Mr. and Mrs. Taylor." I walked to stand beside Philip.

He laid a hand on my shoulder proudly. "This is the friend I wanted you to meet. I owe him my life."

They smiled, thinking it a joke. "Okay, boys, what's going on?"

"Mr. and Mrs. Taylor," I began in the voice I used when talking to employers. "I know you've gone through this once before, but now I fear a third time has to come."

Their looks of amusement faded into ones of apprehension. Mr. Taylor looked at both of us uncertainly. "What's this all about? Last time this happened, you boys proved you were twins. You're not telling us you're triplets, are you?"

"Where's Jesse?" Mrs. Taylor asked, looking around. "If you're not Jesse, where is he?"

"I am Jesse," I assured. They sat back, relieved. "Don't look so happy yet. You are, in a way, parents to triplets." Their expressions turned to astonishment. "I ask you now to prepare yourselves for a shock."

"What is it, boys?"

"Before I go on, I must ask you both to raise your right hand and repeat after me."

"What?"

"If you don't, I'll never be able to tell you about the third son." They shrugged then raised their right hands. Quickly, I swore them into silence as I'd done with Philip. "You know how Philip wouldn't talk about the kidnapping and how he said an agent would contact you later? Well, it's your third son who told him to say that."

I ran my hand through my hair. Why was it so hard to spit it out? This was worse than facing a firing squad, or so it felt. "Look," I finally rushed. "I'm not who you think I am. I *am* Jesse Target, but that's only one part of me. The other part is your third triplet. I'm kind of two people. Jesse Target and Jesse Best."

"Wait right there," Mr. Taylor demanded. "Are you telling us you have a split personality?"

"No, that's not what I'm saying at all! Look, Jesse Target is the boy most see. He's my cover figure. Jesse Best is an undercover detective/secret agent. I'm two people, in that I'm super undercover because of my age. I wouldn't need to be two people if I were twenty-five, but I have to get as close to a normal life as possible because I'm just a kid. School, friends, a home."

"So, you're saying you lead a double life?" Mrs. Taylor clarified.

"That's right. Let me start at the beginning...." I told them everything about how I'd become Jesse Best. They listened patiently the entire time I spoke. "To wrap this up," I said, leaning against the fountain. "I told you all this to say that it was me who found Philip and got him out. I made him promise not to tell you about it so I could. I only pretended to be in Miami."

"Quite an interesting story, Jesse," Mr. Taylor applauded.

"Yes," agreed Mrs. Taylor smiling. "Entertaining."

I smiled in amusement. "You don't believe me, do you?"

They glanced at each other. It was Mr. Taylor who spoke. "I believe you both have been under tremendous strain, and to ease that tension, you imagined an alternate version of the abduction. It's a great story, and I'm glad you were able to find a way to get through the kidnapping's effects together. But I'm sorry, Jesse, you're only fourteen. I'm afraid being an agent and the one to rescue Philip is too hard to believe."

Philip felt rejected by his parents' lack of belief. He slumped in his chair and bowed his head.

I didn't feel rejected. I'd gone through this many times with my employers, and I'd come prepared. "Mr. and Mrs. Taylor, I knew this would be unbelievable and that you would have a hard time accepting it, so I took the liberty of preparing some proofs." I pulled a wallet from my hip pocket and withdrew two items. I handed them to the waiting adults. While they examined them,

I explained their authenticity. "These belonged to my parents; their identification cards. One is my mom's badge for the CIA headquarters, and the other is my dad's detective license." I pulled another card from the wallet and handed it to them. "These are the numbers of the CIA director and agency that licensed my dad. You'll also notice a number that will seem familiar to you because you've called it before—Ace and Daisy's. I wasn't placed at Twin Pines coincidentally. The Jacksons knew my parents and had been acting as my handlers since their deaths." They looked up at me, eyes wide. "Feel free to call any of them and check my facts. They know to expect you." I removed another card. "This is my detective license. Notice it's from the same place as my dad's." I pulled out my last card. "And this is the identification the CIA director gave me when I started working in the field with my mom." I shrugged my shoulders. "You can say this is fake, but on my word of honor, I'm not pretending—I don't have to. My life is exciting enough without adding flare."

They looked up at me, awe filling their faces. "You really are a secret agent," they said in unison.

I nodded. "I am. Not to mention a detective."

"We won't need to talk to anyone," Mr. Taylor told me, handing my things back. "Even if you could make fake identifications that are this good, you couldn't fake the contacts, and I don't think you'd offer them to us if it weren't real. This is amazing, but we believe you."

Philip grinned proudly.

Mrs. Taylor surprised me by pulling me into her arms and hugging me tightly. "Thank you so much for saving Philip! We'll never be able to repay you for this."

"You can, by listening to the rest of my story."

She let me go and sat back. "Of course we will. What else?"

I didn't think of them as my parents, yet I liked them a lot. Knowing that in a few minutes, they might wish never to have met me made a lump come to my throat. I looked away. "You're going to hate me."

This shocked them. "No, Jesse, we could never hate you. You're our son, just as much as Philip is."

"Listen to what I have to tell you before calling me your son. You may want to send me out of your lives forever for what I've caused."

"You're beginning to frighten me. What is it?"

I told them everything about why Philip had been kidnapped. "That's the truth," I ended. "If you hate me, I understand. I'm truly sorry I put Philip in danger. I would have done anything— even surrendering myself to them—to prevent that."

"Jesse, I know you feel responsible for this," Mr. Taylor shook his head, "but you're not. You brought terrorists to justice, saving hundreds of lives. You cannot help that some escaped and came back for revenge, or that they mistook Philip for you. You risked your life then, and you risked it now, when you saved Philip, even though you knew you were the desired target."

I looked him in the eye. "And if he had died, would you be so forgiving?"

Mrs. Taylor spoke slowly, carefully thinking over what she wanted to say. "I think, for a while, I would have been very angry," she admitted honestly. "But only until I realized what I know now, and that is that I love you very much, Jesse." I blinked, kind of surprised because though they'd been calling me their son and treating me like one, they hadn't actually said they loved me. She smiled. "That does surprise you, doesn't it? That I love you. But I truly do. I would never send you out of my life for any reason." She turned to her husband. "Would you, Justin?"

Mr. Taylor shook his head. "Never. We might only have just discovered you, but you're our son, Jesse. I love you, too."

I chewed on my lip a minute. It was great that they could forgive me and love me, but that didn't relieve all my concerns.

Finally, I just asked, "Can you handle my secret life? Can you handle knowing I'm in the crosshairs of a sniper twenty-four-seven? If you can't, I'll have to leave here." I set my jaw determinedly. "I won't give up Jesse Best."

They exchanged glances. "We will *learn* to handle it. Though we may have some rough times, it's very clear that this is who you are. It wouldn't be right to demand you leave it behind simply because we feared for your safety."

Philip jumped in. "Mom, Dad, his safety isn't something you have to worry about—I've seen him in action." He grinned at me. "He lives up to his name. He really is the best."

30
NO MORE LOST

Things began changing around the mansion after my identity was revealed. Security was upgraded to allow me to bring my detective and agent stuff onto the grounds. Before, it hadn't been safe to store classified data on the Taylor estate, so I would have had to return to Twin Pines any time I needed to use my things. Now, that wasn't going to be a problem. The upgrades would also make it safer if other enemies I took down ever decided to come after us. No one questioned it because of Philip's kidnapping.

Another change came in the form of mine and Philip's suite. Mr. and Mrs. Taylor wanted to build a headquarters where I could work without fear of discovery. The employees were given two weeks off, and a team of CIA craftsmen came in to handle the alterations. The bathroom and closet were being downscaled a few feet so that no one would notice the change in size. The space that provided would create a secret room, where I could set up my gear. It would be four feet wide and ten feet deep. The door would be concealed inside the towel closet in the bathroom. It was perfect.

I was really proud of the Taylors; they were handling everything really well. They never failed to behave the same way they had before knowing of their "third son." That's not to say everything stayed the same between us, though.

A week after the upgrades and alterations, the Taylors called me into their private study. As we sat down in comfortable chairs, my thoughts ran wild. After everything they'd done, they weren't going to tell me they'd changed their minds and couldn't handle my secret life, were they? I began to pray that it was something less serious. To stall for time more than anything else, I asked, "I'm not in trouble, am I?"

Mr. Taylor smiled reassuringly. "No, you're not. Ever since the police questioned you, Alicia and I have wanted to talk with you." I relaxed; this couldn't be about Jesse Best, then. Mr. Taylor continued. "We didn't understand just how important this was to you until you were embarrassed when Officer Black asked you about calling us Dad and Mom. Since then, we've been waiting for the right time to speak with you about it."

I started getting nervous again. *They aren't going to tell me I have to start calling them dad and mom, are they? They can't! I won't! I won't pretend like the Targets—my dad and mom—never existed. They raised me as their son for twelve years. I thought they were my blood parents for fourteen years. They are my parents. Blood has nothing to do with it. They're so much a part of who I am. Can't the Taylors understand that?*

"It occurred to us when you first came that we kept saying things like 'the time we lost' and how we wanted to make up for 'lost' time. After you were questioned, we recognized that this attitude came across as if we considered your life with the Targets as a waste. We made it seem as though you had been penalized by not growing up surrounded by the family wealth." He turned to his wife. "Didn't we, Alicia?"

Mrs. Taylor nodded. "We did, and we decided we needed to do something about that." She turned to me, and I was surprised to see tears in her eyes as she took my hand and squeezed it tightly. "You are an incredible boy, Jesse. The Targets were amazing people, and I hope you never think that we despise the time you had with them." She wiped a tear from her eye. "You never said anything, but there were times I could tell you were hurt by the way we continually classified the time you spent with the Targets as lost." Hesitantly, I nodded. She shook her head, swallowing hard. "Oh, Jesse, we never meant to hurt you. I think you knew something we took longer to realize: it was *us* who lost something, not you. You have had two sets of godly parents who love you and want to see you be everything you can be. That's not a loss; that's a gain."

"We have also learned how to be happy about what we lost in not raising you ourselves," Mr. Taylor explained. "We wouldn't have been able to make you everything you are right now." I knew he was talking about Jesse Best. "Alicia and I want you to know that we love you very much, and the 'lost' is gone for good."

I looked from him to Mrs. Taylor. She nodded with a smile. "Gone for good, Jesse. We understand now. What's more, we are proud to have you, Jesse Ethan Target, as our son."

Mr. Taylor nodded. "Philip will carry on the Taylor name, but we want you to fulfill your parents' wish and carry on the Target name. Today, Jesse, we give you your name to hold and cherish forever. Wear your name with the same pride you always have."

I swallowed hard and blinked back tears. "Thank you both so much.... Will you, will you talk to the employees about this? They keep calling me Jesse Taylor."

"Oh, Jesse, I'm sorry. We didn't know," Mr. Taylor lamented. "I'll tell them you are remaining with the name Target."

"Thank you." I looked up quickly, feeling like I had to explain. "It's not that I don't want to be part of your family—"

"The Targets were your parents," Mrs. Taylor cut in. "At first, it was hard to understand how you could love them when we were your real mother and father, but now I see that's factually sound, but not emotionally. The Targets were your *real* parents. And now I understand even better why you love them so much."

I had been trained to handle anything like a pro, but even a pro couldn't have helped the tear that slipped from the corner of my eye and down my cheek. The Taylors had just given me a key to a door I thought they were going to lock forever: the door to my past. I would no longer have to worry about slipping and saying something about my parents because now they understood. They were even giving me the right to keep my name!

I got up and hugged each of them. "Thank you so much for understanding. I love you both, I really do."

"We love you too, Jesse."

I got a phone call the following Saturday; it was Daisy and Ace. They wanted to come visit me this afternoon. Something about some letters for me. Excitedly, I asked Philip if he thought his parents would mind. He said he didn't.

Daisy and Ace came an hour after lunch. The Taylors were thrilled to see them again and offered to show them around the mansion. Before they started their tour, Daisy handed me a packet of letters. I read the name on the recipient's address: Tim Strickland. While they headed to the golf carts, I went to my room to catch up on some top-secret corresponding. Philip followed me.

"I'm getting the strangest exciting feeling," he said, plopping down on his bed facing me.

I raised an eyebrow. "Oh?"

"What are those?"

I stuck them under my pillow. "Sorry, Philip. Confidential."

He grinned. "Then I'm out of here. I don't want to interfere with a *CIA agent*." He mouthed the last words.

I shook my head, grinning at his over precautiousness. I was going to like him knowing I was an agent just because of his reactions. Once the door was closed securely behind him, I opened the first of six letters; it was from Preetah. I read it slowly, remembering every detail of the case. Her closing words were her usual: "*I thank my God upon every remembrance of you.*"

Next, I read the letters from the twins. They told me how they were doing and how excited they were to be going to summer camp next year—their first time. They closed their letter with: "*Always happy, always helping. We love and miss you, Us.*"

The letter from the spy was trickiest to read. He always wrote in code to pass on his latest intel. I wrote down his messages, then went to my little Mexican friend.

He wrote his letter in Spanish—no problem for me. I knew the language like a native. He closed his letter with,"*Hasta el aproximo, mi gran amigo.*"

Lastly, I opened my newest pen pal's letter. Baldwin had written just as I'd told him to in the letter I'd given him at the airport. It was just a short letter, more of a note. It said:

Hi, Tim. I'm so glad I got your address! I really enjoyed our time together. I look forward to our correspondence with great expectation. Time is short, so I have to go.

Your friend forever, Baldwin.

P.S. I think I will take you up on your idea. Writing books sounds interesting. Who knows? Maybe someday, when we're both old and gray, I may even write the story of how we met.

Grinning, I put the letter back in its envelope. Someday, he really might take our case and turn it into a book. Maybe, when they were no longer classified, I'd share all my case files with him. Who knew? He might even make a hit out of one of them.